記得你个好

Your Goodness is Always on My Mind

記得你的好

詩畫選集

含樂譜/MV

這生人个
情同愛
獻分親愛个你

倨
永久
記得你个好

lifetime
affection and love
for my dear

I
always
remember how good you are

這輩子的
情與愛
獻給親愛的你

我
永遠
記得你的好

目　錄

詩歌篇

臍帶情

一片真心

尋與思

想望

在山里對岸想汝

客語

倕在山里對岸遙望
卑南大溪在眼前打橫過
食中央山脈个奶汁
接海岸山脈个汗水
闊野野个大河壩　緊滾緊闊　緊滾緊闊

普悠瑪勇士走到比弓箭還較遽
手一伸
窩湖水就直洩入海
英雄的手尾力削開崩崗石壁
將一條銀帶拉向太平洋

山當近　海當近　人也當近
近到聽得著偃俚个心跳摎夢想

卑南溪唱等思戀歌
倕在山里个對岸想汝

油畫
50F
116.5X91.0cm

~ Miss You on the Bank Across from Shanli ~

On the bank across from Shanli look I into the distance,
The Beinan River's expanse in front.
Weaned on the milk of the Central Mountain Range
Embraced by the sweat of the Coastal Mountain Rangc
Always tumbling wide and far the gaping valley is forever vast.

Puyuma warriors run faster than arrows.
Like their outstretched hands,
Runs the water of the lakes into the ocean.
The mighty hands of heroes chop the cliffs apart,
Drawing a silver belt to the Pacific.

Mountains and ocean are nestled close, as are people.
So close that we could hear the heartbeats and dreams of each other.

The Beinan River sings songs of love and longing.
Missing you stand I on the bank across from Shanli.

在山里對岸想你

華語

我在山里對岸遙望
卑南大溪橫亙在眼前
食中央山脈的奶水
接海岸山脈的汗水
寬闊的河谷　一直翻滾　一直遼闊　繼續寬闊

普悠瑪勇士跑得比弓箭還快
手一伸
湖水就直奔入海
英雄的手勁削開斷崖赤壁
將一條銀帶拉向太平洋

山很近　海很近　人也很近
近到可以聽見我們彼此的心跳與夢想

卑南溪唱著思戀歌
我在山里對岸想你

在山里對岸想汝

原唱：G小調

詞：彭歲玲
曲：羅思容

偓 在 山 里 對 岸 遙 望 卑 南 大 溪 在

眼 前 打 橫 過 食 中 央 山 脈 个 奶 汁 接

海岸山脈 个 汗 水 闊野 野 个 大 河 壩 啊

緊 滾 緊 闊 緊 滾 緊 闊 (間奏)

普 悠 瑪 个 勇 士 走 到 比 弓 箭 還 較 遠 手 一

23
伸 窩湖 水 就 直洩 入 海

30
英 雄个水 尾 力 削 開 崩崗石 壁 將 一條

38
銀帶 拉 向 太 平 洋 (間奏)

48
山 當近 海 當近 人也 當 近

54
近到 聽得 著 偲俚 个心 跳 摎夢 想

60
卑 南溪 唱 等 思 戀 歌 哪唉 喲

64
倕在 山里 个對 岸 想汝 (間奏)

70
山 當近 海 當近 人乜 當 近

76
近到 聽得 著 偲俚 个心跳 摎夢 想

82
卑 南溪 唱 等 思 戀 歌 哪唉 喲

86
倕在 山里 个對 岸 想汝 想汝 想汝 伊

靚靚茶香情

客語

青山岈岡在眼前
白雲共下向前行

（一）
揚蝶仔著等花衫尋花蜜
鳥仔牽聲唱山歌
蟻公覓做無時閒
山狗太緊頷頭　緊講幾多點
肩頭擔竿　逐等日頭花

嘿咻　嘿咻　嘿得咻
汗水　涔 涔 流
山路　穩 穩 行

嘿咻　嘿咻　嘿得咻
汗水　涔 涔 流
山路　穩 穩 行

附註：這首詩歌是為奉茶文化編寫的，描述辛勤的過路人走在山路看見的情景，在奉茶亭喝了好心人家準備的茶水，體會茶香及人情味，於是充滿希望邁開腳步繼續向前走。

（口白）

嘿～恁早　　嘿～仰恁煞猛呢

來來來

歇睏一下　尞涼　食碗茶來

（二）

好心人家　貼心善良

就像日頭暖心肝

甜甜个相借問

靚靚个笑容

就像春風帶花香

心靚

茶香

分人心花開

甘甜

情緣

永難忘

水彩

42.0X29.7cm

（口白）
哇～還甜哪　　哇～仰恁貼心
心肝恁好
來去喲～　孩起春風起腳行囉～

（三）
揚尾仔摘等春風咪咪仔笑
鳥仔雙飛望連理
望得兩人結成緣
天頂个天弓啊　顯出真多彩
肩頭擔竿 逐等日頭花

嘿咻　嘿咻　嘿得咻
汗水　湉 湉 流
茶香　日 日 有

嘿咻　嘿咻　嘿得咻
汗水　湉 湉 流
豐收　年 年 有

~ Wonderful Affections for Fragrant Tea ~

Stand verdant hills before my eyes.
Together with white clouds, forward I move.

A.
Dressed in colorful clothes, butterflies look for nectar.
Raising voices high, the birds sing mountain songs.
With no break, the ants work hard.
Asking what time it is, the mountain lizard nods his head.
The pole on my shoulders runs after sunbeams through clouds.

Hexiu hexiu hedexiu
The sweat is dripping down and down.
On the mountain roads, I walk steady and slow.

Hexiu hexiu hedexiu
The sweat is dripping down and down.
On the mountain roads, I walk steady and slow.

(Addressing)

Hey, good morning. Hey, How come so diligent!

Come over here!

Take a break, relax in the shade, have a cup of tea.

B.

Good-hearted people, considerate and kind.

Just like the sunshine, warming my heart.

A sweet hello,

A pretty smile,

Just like spring breeze, carrying floral scents.

Beautiful heart,

Fragrant tea,

Make my heart bloom with blossoms.

Pleasant sweet

Affections,

I forget not.

(Addressing)

Wow! So sweet! Wow! How come so considerate!

With such a kind heart.

I'll leave now. Carrying a spring breeze, I keep going, marching forward.

C

Embracing the spring breeze, the butterflies smile.

Looking for matrimony, two birds fly together.

Looking forward to seeing the two be as one.

Oh, rainbow in the sky, magnificent colors you do show.

The pole on my shoulders, runs after sunbeams through the clouds.

Hexiu hexiu hedexiu

The sweat is dripping down and down.

Fragrant tea comes day by day.

Hexiu hexiu hedexiu

The sweat is dripping down and down.

Big harvest comes year by year.

美好茶香情

華語

青翠山岡在眼前
白雲一起向前行

(一)
蝴蝶穿著彩衣尋花蜜
鳥兒啼聲唱山歌
螞蟻勤做沒停歇
山蜥蜴點點頭　現在是幾點了
肩上扁擔　追著日頭花

嘿咻　嘿咻　嘿得咻
汗水　答 答 流
山路　穩 穩 走

嘿咻　嘿咻　嘿得咻
汗水　答 答 流
山路　穩 穩 走

(口白)

嘿 ~ 早啊　　嘿 ~ 怎麼這麼勤勞啊

來來來

休息一下　歇涼　喝碗茶

(二)

好心人家　貼心善良

就像陽光暖心頭

甜甜的打招呼

美美的笑容

就像春風帶花香

心美

茶香

讓人心花開

甘甜

情緣

永難忘

（口白）
哇～好甜哪　　哇～怎麼這麼貼心
心腸這麼好
來去喲～　挑起春風 邁開腳步 向前走囉～

（三）
蜻蜓抱著春風微微笑
鳥兒雙飛盼連理
盼望兩人結成雙
天上的彩虹啊　顯出真多彩
肩上扁擔 追著日頭花

嘿咻　嘿咻　嘿得咻
汗水　答 答 流
茶香　日 日 有

嘿咻　嘿咻　嘿得咻
汗水　答 答 流
豐收　年 年 有

靚靚茶香情

原唱：E調

詞：彭歲玲
曲：許良華

♩= 102

青 山 屻 岡　喔　在 眼　前　哪　白 雲

6 共 下　啊　向 前　行 哪

13 揚　蝶 仔 著 等 花 衫　尋 花　蜜　鳥　仔　牽　聲

17 唱 山 歌　蟻 公　覓 做　無 時 閒　山 狗 太　緊 頷 頭

25 緊 講　幾 多　點　肩　頭　擔　竿　逐 等　日 頭 花

32
嘿 咻 嘿 咻 嘿得咻 汗水 湁湁流 山路 穩穩行
40
嘿 咻 嘿 咻 嘿得咻 汗水 湁湁流 山路 穩穩行
48
8
（間奏）嘿~恁早 嘿~仰恁煞猛呢
來來來 歇睏一下 尞涼 食碗茶來
好 心 人 家
57
貼 心 善 良 就 像日 頭 暖 心肝 甜 甜个相借問
63
靚 靚个笑 容 就像春風帶 花 香 心靚 茶 香
69
分 人心 花 開 甘 甜 情 緣 永 難 忘

75
8
（間奏）哇~還甜哪　哇~仰恁貼心
心肝恁好　來去喲~　孩起春風起腳行囉~
揚　尾　仔　捕　等　春　風
84
咪咪仔 笑　鳥 仔 雙 飛　望連理　望得　兩人　結成緣
93
天頂个　天弓啊　顯出　真多　彩
98
肩　頭　擔　竿　逐　等　日頭花
102
嘿 咻 嘿 咻　嘿得咻　汗 水　溚溚流　茶香　日日有
110
嘿 咻 嘿 咻　嘿得咻　汗 水　溚溚流　豐收　年年有

記得你个好

客語

有一日，你可能喊毋出偃个名
毋過，
偃還會陪你共食朝，陪你散步
你毋記得偃無相干，偃記得你就好
就像朝晨葉尾打眼晟光該粒露水
明知會消失乜甘願擁有～最靚个甘甜

有一日，你可能喊毋出偃个名
毋過，
偃還會摎你放心肝，摎你講話
你毋記得偃無相干，偃記得你就好
就像暗夜星光陪等月光，共下行過
無論到哪位乜一定永久～記得你个好
啊～記得你个好

水彩
39.5X27.2cm

~ Your Goodness is Always on My Mind ~

One day, you may not be able to call my name.
Yet,
I'll still have breakfast with you, take a walk with you.
It matters not you recognize me no more, for I remember you.
Just like the crystal clear morning dew on the leaf tip,
holding on to this fairest sweetness, though knowing it, too, will vanish.

One day, you may not be able to call my name.
Yet,
I'll still keep you in my heart, talk to you.
It matters not you recognize me no more, for I remember you.
Just like the stars accompanying the moon, walking in the sky through the night.
No matter where we reach, your goodness is always on my mind.
Ah~ Your goodness is always on my mind.

記得你的好

華語

有一天，你可能叫不出我的名
但是，
我還會陪你吃早餐，陪你散步
你不認得我沒關係，我記得你就好
就像晨間葉稍晶瑩透光那顆露珠
明知將消失也寧願擁有 ~ 最美的甘甜

有一天，你可能叫不出我的名
但是，
我還會把你放心裡，跟你講話
你不認得我沒關係，我記得你就好
就像夜空星星陪伴月亮，一起走過
無論到哪裡也一定永遠 ~ 記得你的好
啊 ~ 記得你的好

記得你个好

原唱：D調

詞：彭歲玲
曲：許良華

(一) 有 一 日 你可能 喊 毋 出 俚 个 名
(二) 有 一 日 你可能 喊 毋 出 俚 个 名

毋 過 俚還會 陪 你 共 食 朝 陪
毋 過 俚還會 摎 你 放 心 肝 摎

你 散 步 你 毋 記 得 俚 無 相 干
你 講 話 你 毋 記 得 俚 無 相 干

俚 記 得 你 就 好 就
俚 記 得 你 就 好 就

17
像 朝 晨 葉 尾 打 眼 晟 光 該 粒
像 暗 夜 星 光 陪 等 月 光 共 下
21
露 水 明 知 會 消 失 乜 甘 願 擁
行 過 無 論 到 哪 位 乜 一 定 永
25
有 最 靚 个 甘 甜
久 記 得 你 个 好
29
啊 啊 啊 最 靚 个 甘 甜
啊 啊 啊 記 得 你 个 好

身影

客語

田坵
有阿爸个身影
寒往暑來，青溜溜个禾仔既經毋識俚个阿爸
白雲啊！你還記得
一個毋驚魍神个男仔人
揹等簝公，半夜行在田脣項，捉蛤蟆
愛分妹仔食，醫身項个長薯仔

河壩
有阿姆个身影
春去冬來，流不停个河水既經毋識俚个阿姆
白雲啊！你還記得
一個毋驚寒个婦人家
揹等菜籃，打早跍在河壩脣，洗衫褲
愛分屋下人著一身清香淨俐

水彩
39.5X27.2cm

火車路
有阿爸个身影
花開花謝，靚呢呢个路脣花既經毋識佢个阿爸
白雲啊！你還記得
一個盡惜子个男仔人
揹等妹仔，拚命走過火車窿，趕車枋
愛分醫生看，發燒發病个細孲仔

山崎頂
有阿姆个身影
一季換一季，打當結个刺波仔，既經毋識佢个阿姆
白雲啊！你還記得
一個盡煞猛个婦人家
帶等刀嫲，歸下晝鑽到樹林肚，撿樵
愛分灶頭起火，煮出燒暖个飯菜

白雲啊白雲
淨你知得
多彩个天弓
掛等
多彩个思念
該係
永恆个靚

< 以詩入歌 >　　阿爸个身影（客語）

阿爸个身影　無限思念
阿爸个身影　春去冬來
青溜溜个禾仔啊
既經毋識偓阿爸
月光啊 ~ 你敢會知得
野鳥仔啊 ~ 你敢會還記得
一個毋驚鬾神个男仔人
暗夜揹等篡公　去捉蛤蟆
啊　啊　啊 ~~~
為醫細孲仔个長著仔
行田脣，毋知風寒
一個毋驚鬾神个男仔人
佢係偓个阿爸

Silhouette

The field
Contains the silhouette of my father.
Winter has left and come summer days, the glossy green rice has recognized my father no more.
Oh white clouds! Can you recall
A man who fears no demons nor ghosts,
Walking on the farm ridges, with a bamboo basket on his back, trying to catch toads.
For the healing of his daughter's pimples.

The river
Contains the silhouette of my mother.
Spring has left and come winter days, the endlessly running river has recognized my mother no more.
Oh white clouds! Can you recall
A woman who fears no cold,

Crouching by the river in early morning, with a vegetable basket on her back, washing clothes.
For the tidyness of her family's clothes.

The rail
Contains the silhouette of my father.
The flowers have blossomed and withered, the tender delicate wild flowers have recognized my father no more.
Oh white clouds! Can you recall
A man who adores his kids the most,
Running through the rail tunnels, with his daughter on his back, trying to catch the train.

For bringing the fevered sick kid to the doctor.

The hill
Contains the silhouette of my mother.
One season has left and comes another one, the fruitful wild strawberries have recognized my mother no more.
Oh white clouds! Can you recall
A hard-working woman,
Seeking through the woods the whole afternoon, with a hatchet in her hands, collecting firewood.
For lighting the stove to prepare hot dishes,

Oh white clouds,
Only you can see it through.
How the colorful rainbow
Is draped
With colorful memories.
That is
The beauty of eternity.

<Song lyric from the poem> The Silhouette of My Father

The silhouette of my father, forever do I long.

The silhouette of my father, spring has left and come winter days.

Oh, glossy green rice

Could recognize my father no more.

Oh, the moon, do you know?

Oh, wild birds, can you recall?

A man who fears no demons nor ghosts,

Carrying a bamboo basket at midnight, trying to catch toads.

Ah Ah Ah ~~~

For healing the pimples of his kid.

Walking on the farm ridges, fearing no chill nor cold,

A man who fears no demons nor ghosts.

He is the father of mine.

田園
有阿爸的身影
寒往暑來，綠油油的稻子已經不認識我的阿爸
白雲啊！你還記得
一個不怕魑魅魍魎的男人
揹著竹簍，半夜走在田埂，捉青蛙
要給女兒吃，醫身上的青春痘

溪流
有媽媽的身影
春去冬來，流不停的溪水已經不認識我的媽媽
白雲啊！你還記得
一個不怕冷的婦人家
揹著菜籃，清早蹲在溪流旁，洗衣
要給家人穿一身清香淨俐

火車路
有阿爸的身影
花開花謝，嬌豔的路邊花已經不認識我的阿爸

白雲啊！你還記得
一個最疼孩子的男人
揹著女兒，拚命跑過火車隧道，趕車班
要給醫生看，發燒生病的小孩

山坡上
有媽媽的身影
一季換一季，果實累累的野草莓，已經不認識我的媽媽
白雲啊！你還記得
一個最勤勞的婦人家
帶著柴刀，整個下午鑽到樹林裡，撿柴
要給灶起火，煮出溫暖的飯菜

白雲啊白雲
只你了解
多彩的彩虹
掛著
多彩的思念
那是
永恆的美

< 以詩入歌 >　　阿爸个身影（華語）

阿爸的身影　　無限思念
阿爸的身影　　春去冬來
綠油油的稻子啊
已經不認識我阿爸
月兒啊 ~ 你可知道
野鳥啊 ~ 你可還記得
一個不怕魑魅魍魎的男人
半夜揹著竹簍　去捉青蛙
啊　啊　啊 ~~~
為醫小孩的青春痘
走田埂，不知風寒
一個不怕魑魅魍魎的男人
他是我的阿爸

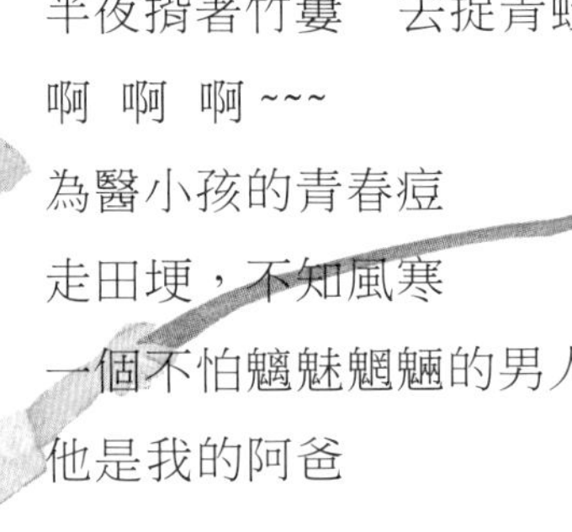

阿爸个身影

原唱：D調

詞：彭歲玲
曲：許良華

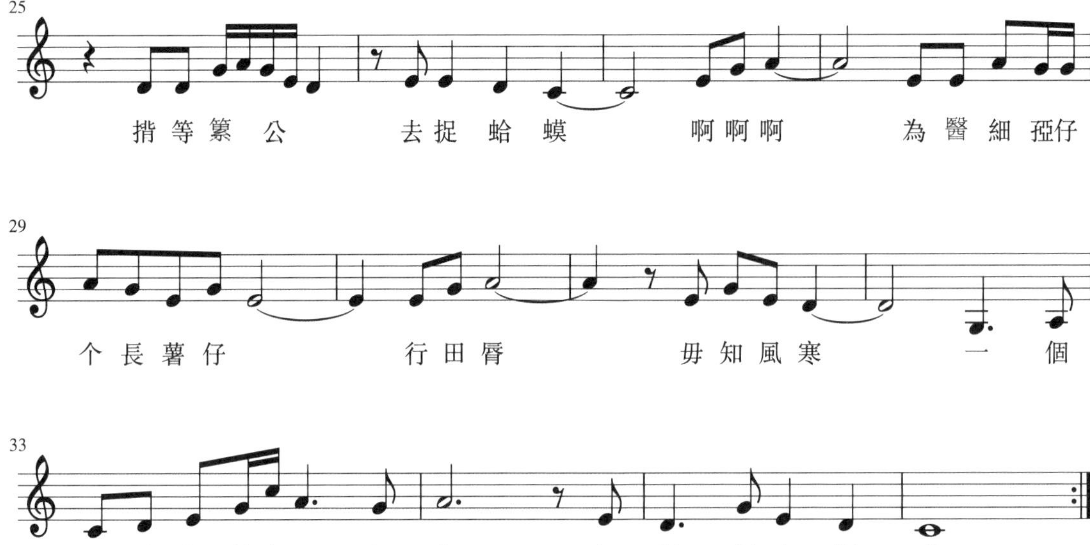
25
揹 等 簝 公 去 捉 蛤 蟆 啊 啊 啊 為 醫 細 孲仔
29
个 長 薯 仔 行 田 脣 毋 知 風 寒 一 個
33
毋 驚 魍 神 个 男 仔 人 佢 係 𠊎 个 阿 爸

有你在身邊

客語

女：俚想做牽牛花 開到哪位都恁靚
你係行在路項 隨時都會看著俚
男：你若係牽牛花 俚就變成微風
輕輕圍在四方 陪在你身邊
合：啊～牽牛花 啊～都恁靚
有你在俚身邊 世界仰恁靚

男：俚想愛做月光 掛在天頂照你
你係臥頭看俚 俚會笑咪咪
女：你若係月光 俚就變成嫦娥
飛到你个心肚 千里共嬋娟
合：啊～月光 啊～照四方
有你在俚身邊 世界恁美好

對白 1：(女) 你今晡日愛煮麼个好食个啊？
(男) 做麼个輪著俚煑啊？
(女) 你煑个較好食啊！
(男) 好啦！好啦！
對白 2：(女) 你著恁派頭愛去哪位啊？
(男) 愛去儘採行行啊 ~
(女) 儘採行？愛去哪仰毋講清楚來？

女 : 俚想做火焰蟲　飛到哪位都矖光
你係看著俚　就會又笑又歡喜
男 : 你若係火焰蟲　俚就變成該燈籠
摎等一矖一矖个光　共下照光明
合 : 啊 ~ 火焰蟲　啊 ~ 照光明
有你在我身邊　　世界都盡好　　世界都盡好

水彩
39.5X27.2cm

With You By My Side

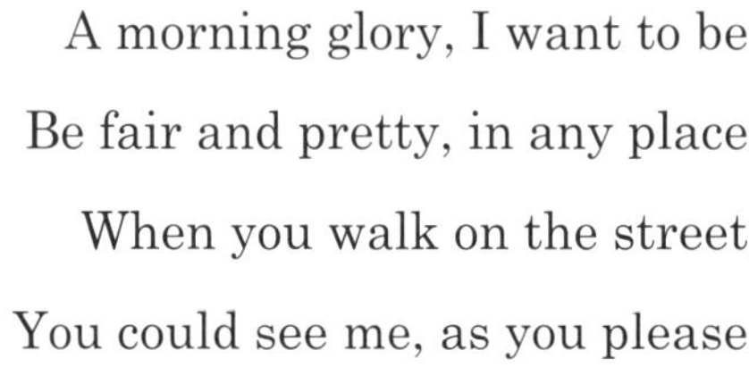

A morning glory, I want to be.
Be fair and pretty, in any place.
When you walk on the street,
You could see me, as you please.

If you were a morning glory,
A breeze, I would be.
Circling you, gently,
By your side, I'd be.

Oh, morning glory! Oh, how pretty!
With you by my side.
How wonderful the world is!

The moon, I want to be,
Shining on you, from the sky.
When you raise your head and look up,
At you, I shall smile.

If you were the moon,
Chang 'e, I would be.
To you, I do fly,
Be heavenly together, through thousands of miles.

Oh, the moon! Oh, shining all the way!
With you by my side.
How wonderful the world is!

Dialogue 1: (Woman) What delicious food are you going to cook today?
(Man) Why is it my turn to cook?
(Woman) Because your food is more delicious!
Dialogue 2: (Woman) Where are you going in such a handsome outfit?
(Man) Just walk around.
(Woman) Just walk around? Why don't you make it clear where you are going?

A firefly, I want to be.
Be twinkly glowing, wherever I fly.
When you spot me,
How amazed and happy, you would be.

If you were a firefly,
That lantern, I would be.
Carrying flickering lights,
Shining together, all the nights.

Oh, firefly! Oh, shining light!
With you by my side.
How wonderful the world is!
How wonderful the world is!

有你在身旁

華語

我想當牽牛花
開在哪兒都漂亮
當你走在路上
隨時都會看見我

你若是牽牛花
我就變成微風
輕輕環繞四方
陪在你身邊

啊 ~~~ 牽牛花　　啊 ~~~ 多漂亮
有你在我身旁
世界多美好

我想當月亮
掛在天邊照亮你
當你抬頭高望
我就會微笑

你若是月亮
我就變成嫦娥
飛到你的懷抱
千里共嬋娟

啊 ~~~ 月亮　　啊 ~~~ 照四方
有你在我身旁
世界多美好

對白 1：(女) 你今天要煮什麼好吃的啊？
(男) 為什麼輪到我煑啊？
(女) 你煑的比較好吃啊！
(男) 好啦！好啦！
對白 2：(女) 你穿這麼帥要去哪裡啊？
(男) 要去隨意走走 ~
(女) 隨意走？要去哪裡怎麼不講清楚啊？

我想當螢火蟲
飛到哪兒都閃亮
當你看見了我
就會既驚喜又開心

你若是螢火蟲
我就變成那燈籠
提著一閃一閃的光
一起放光明

啊 ~~~ 螢火蟲　　啊 ~~~ 放光明
有你在我身旁
世界多美好
世界多美好

有你在身邊

原唱：D調

詞：彭歲玲
曲：許良華

（前奏）

5 （一）女：亻厓 想 做 牽 牛 花 開 到 哪 位 都 恁 靚

9 你 若 行 在 路 頂 隨 時 都 會 看 著 亻厓

13 男：你 若 係 牽 牛 花 亻厓 就 變 成 微 風

17 輕 輕 圍 在 四 方 陪 在 你 身 邊

21
合：啊 牽 牛 花 啊 都 恁 靚
25
有 你在 𠊎 身 邊 世界仰 恁 靚
29
（二）男：𠊎想 愛做 月 光 掛 在天頂照 你
33
你 係臥 頭 看 𠊎 𠊎會笑 咪 咪
37
女：你若 係月 光 𠊎 就變成嫦 娥 飛 到你 个 心 肚
43
千里共 嬋 娟 合：啊 月 光

47
啊 照 四 方 有 你 在 侹 身 邊
51
9
世 界 恁 美 好
(對白)
62
(間奏)
66
(三)女：侹 想 做 火 焰 蟲 飛 到 哪 位 都 矚光
70
你 係 看 著 侹 就 會 又 笑 又 歡 喜
74
男：你 若 係 火 焰 蟲 侹 就 變 成 該 燈 籠

對白 1：（女）你今晡日愛煮麼个好食个啊？
（男）做麼个輪著倨煮啊？
（女）你煮个較好食啊！
（男）好啦！好啦！

對白 2：（女）你著恁派頭愛去哪位啊？
（男）愛去儘採行行啊～
（女）儘採行？愛去哪仰毋講清楚來？

客語

go~~go go go

go~~go go go

阿姆逐日像練聲胲樣仔

大嬤牯聲嘍雞仔

go~~go go go

go~~go go go

阿姆嘍雞仔聲長長

黏黏个牽聲黏上天

黏著飛過个白雲還過牽絲

這片黏著雞嬤蟲　該片黏著草蜢仔

黏來黏去

黏轉屋前、屋背、山排、山窩

滿哪仔絡食个雞仔

油畫

25P

80.0X60.5cm

暗微濛个雞寮
麼个都毋驚　就驚臭青嫲
夜風唱起催眠曲
食飽夜个雞仔目絲絲　恬恬企好位所
恬肅肅个禾埕暗摸胥疏
阿姆麼个都毋愁　就愁轉夜个人
月光擎起電火
照等轉夜个路

go~~go go go
雞仔煞猛食　食蟲仔、食石頭、食春風
go~~go go go
阿姆煞猛畜　畜雞仔、畜豬仔、畜一群大細
風講　這屋下人
麼个都有
麼个都無驚

~ Mother Feeding Chickens ~

go~~go go go

go~~go go go

Everyday, as if warming up her voice,

Out loud, mother calls the chickens.

go~~go go go

go~~go go go

When mother calls the chickens, her voice lasts very long.

Long and sticky, the voice sticks to the sky.

It sticks to the flying white clouds and draws a long silk,

It sticks to beetle larvae here and sticks to grasshoppers there.

Sticking here and there.

It sticks back to the front yard, backyard, slope, mountain col,

And the chickens looking for food, everywhere.

Dusky chicken coop
Fears nothing, but the King Ratsnake.
The night breeze sings a lullaby.
Quietly seated in the place, with full stomach the chickens close their eyes.
Stealthily quiet, the yard is pitch black.
Mother worries for nothing, but the home comer at night.
Moonlight raises the lamp,
Shining on the road back home at night.

go~~go go go
go~~go go go
Chickens feed ceaselessly on worms, pebbles, and the spring breeze.
go~~go go go
go~~go go go
Mother raises ceaselessly chickens, pigs, and a bunch of kids.
The wind says, this family
Has everything,
And nothing to fear.

母親餵雞

華語

go~~go go go

go~~go go go

母親每天像練開嗓一樣

大聲召喚雞

go~~go go go

go~~go go go

母親召喚雞的聲音很長很長

黏黏的拉長的聲音黏上天

黏到飛過的白雲又再拉長牽絲

這邊黏到雞母蟲 那邊黏到蚱蜢

黏來黏去

黏回屋前、屋後、山坡、山坳

到處覓食的雞

昏暗的雞寮
什麼都不怕　就怕王錦蛇
夜風唱起催眠曲
吃飽的雞瞇著眼睛　安靜的站好位置
靜悄悄的庭院黑漆漆的
母親什麼都不憂慮　就憂慮夜歸的人
月光舉起電燈
照著夜歸的路

go~~go go go
雞勤勞食　食蟲子、食石頭、食春風
go~~go go go
母親勤勞養　養雞、養豬、養一群小孩
風說　這家人
什麼都有
什麼都不怕

揣頭嬰兒仔

客語

阿姆个背囊
係嬰兒仔在田坵肚搖來搖去个眠床
撩人个日頭
吵醒入覺个嬰兒仔
癮奶食个噭聲
迴過山谷　映過山崗
阿姆解開盤身个背帶
搧出合等汗水个奶汁分嬰兒仔食

冇衫肚个奶臊
餳來揚蝶仔
想食無共樣个花香
嬰兒仔兩隻手擛啊擛
奶水飽足就盡想飛上天

番薯改好
嬰兒仔放入菜籃肚
一頭番薯一頭子
肩頭个擔竿 xim　啊 xim
纘頭攬髻个頭那毛乜毋知
算來係拿番薯摎嬰兒仔掵頭
也係將嬰兒仔摎番薯掵頭

細孲仔一個一個蓄
擔頭一擔一擔孩
阿姆孩起个人生
歲月个皺痕乜毋知
算來係歸日个無閒來掵頭青春
也係拿青春來掵頭日夜个無閒

阿姆淨知
掵頭个嬰兒仔
愛遽遽生出翼胛飛上天

水彩
42.0X29.7cm

Baby in the Shoulder Pole Basket

Mother's back
Is the swinging cradle of the baby on the farm.
The teasing sun
Wakes up the sleeping baby.
And the crying sound for milk
Echoes in the valley, across the hills.
Untying the sashes around her body, the mother
Breastfeeds her baby, the milk mixed with sweat.

The milk aroma in the swaddling
Attracts butterflies,
Who are looking for different floral scents.
Waving both hands, the baby,
Longs to fly up to the sky, once sated with milk.

Dug are the sweet potatoes.
Inside the basket is the baby.
Sweet potatoes in one end, baby in the other one.
Bending is the pole on the shoulders.
Unaware is the disheveled hair.
Whether sweet potatoes are used to balance with baby,
Or baby is used to balance with sweet potatoes?

Children are raised, one after another.
Baskets are carried, one by one.
The life carried by mother,
Unaware are wrinkles of the age.
Whether all-day chores are used to balance with youth,
Or youth is used to balance with day and night chores?

Mother knows only
The baby in her shoulder pole basket
Shall quickly grow a pair of wings, flying to the sky.

平衡擔子的嬰兒

華語

母親的背
是嬰兒在田園裡搖來搖去的眠床
逗弄人的日頭
吵醒熟睡的嬰兒
喝奶癮的哭聲
迴過山谷　映過山崗
母親解開環繞身上的背帶
掏出和著汗水的奶汁給嬰兒食

襁褓裡的奶臊
吸引來蝴蝶
想吃不一樣的花香
嬰兒兩隻手揮舞
奶水飽足就極想飛上天

番薯挖好
嬰兒放入菜籃裡
一頭番薯一頭孩子
肩上的扁擔彎啊彎
披頭散亂的頭髮也不知
到底是拿番薯來和嬰兒平衡
還是將嬰兒來和番薯平衡

小孩一個一個養
擔頭一擔一擔挑
母親挑起的人生
歲月的皺痕也不知
到底是整日的忙碌來平衡青春
還是拿青春來平衡日夜的忙碌

母親只知
平衡擔子的嬰兒
要快快生出翅膀飛上天

金色个恬靜

客語

佢毋知別人喊佢麼个名
毋過　偃一直摎佢喊做　寧靜湖
佢溫柔恬靜
恬恬仔陪在活水湖唇
毋管別位係仰般鬧棚做戲
佢還係
恬靜到連倒影肚个鳥仔聲
都聽得著
水面紋路輕輕仔配合節奏
連微風都躡腳尾行過

從唇項个觀潮橋看過去
就係闊野野个太平洋
你會看著
臨暗仔　勇敢个人落海掖網打魚
你會看著
朝晨頭　相愛个人牽手看日出

油畫
30F
91.0X72.5cm

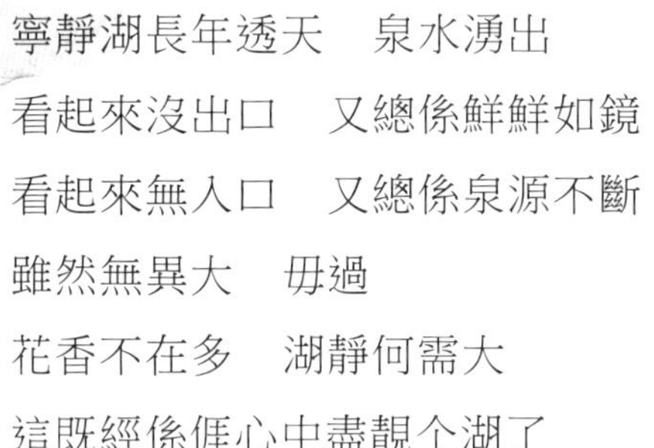

寧靜湖長年透天　泉水湧出
看起來沒出口　又總係鮮鮮如鏡
看起來無入口　又總係泉源不斷
雖然無異大　毋過
花香不在多　湖靜何需大
這既經係佢心中盡靚个湖了

湖水摎星光
共下
行過春天、行過熱天
秋天呢？
秋天个蟬仔聲講等
摎森林个緣分　摎大地个生養
寒天呢？
寒天淨會在你無想行出來該時節正有

湖面天頂高　星光矖啊矖
你看該粒細細个
分偃想起細孲仔轉屋
會捲掷草　會共下有講有笑
星光將卵黃色个燒暖　矖啊矖

你看該粒較遠个
像聽著吾哥摎偃講
老妹，係有事愛記得轉來尋阿哥喔
星光將柑仔色个感動　矖啊矖

你看該粒有一息遠个
像看著遠方个阿姊
逐擺見面喊偃莫再大箍囉　還緊夾菜分偃
星光將粉色个關心　矖啊矖

再看該粒暗微光个
分偃想起夥房老人家
時常尋毋著大紅色个衫　時常喊毋出子孫个名
還係緊唸~仰毋遽遽去煮飯分大家食飽來呢？
星光將灰濛灰濛淡黃色个毋盼得　矖啊矖

你再看該粒盡近个
想起為心愛个人寫个詩
心肝肚个話　化作音符為佢唱出
星光將紅炣紅炣个
幸福　矖啊矖

還有還有
你再看該盡遠盡遠个
像看著阿爸阿姆在遠遠天頂高
總係看等妹仔有麼个湛斗事
脣口恁多恁多个金色星仔群
全無講話　陪在天邊笑咪咪仔　矖啊矖

暗夜星光緊矖
各種色共下映照下來
湖面比黃金還較金
心肝肚个愛
就像湖肚个泉眼
湧出
秋湖在金色中

~ Golden Tranquility ~

What name she is called, I've never known.
Yet, Lake of Tranquility, is how I call.
Tender and calm, as she is.
Next to Flowing Lake, quietly she sits.
No matter how frisky frolicking elsewhere is,
She remains
Quiet, that even the chirps of reflected birds
Are clearly heard.
Gently, the water texture follows the rhythm,
Even a soft wind passes tiptoed.

Gazing from the Tide-Watching Bridge nearby,
The immense Pacific Ocean is beheld.
Where you could see
Brave men in the sea, throwing cast nets, at dusk.
Where you could see
Lovers holding hands, watching sunrise, at dawn.

A spring gushes in Lake of Tranquility, all year round.
No apparent exit, yet clear as a mirror it is.
No apparent entrance, yet endlessly it flows.
Covering no big space, though,
The number matters not when the flowers smell nice; the size matters not when the lake is quiet.
This has been the most beautiful lake, in my heart.

Lake water and star light,
Along with each other,
Going through spring, going through summer.
How about autumn?
The cicadas of autumn are talking
About their connections with the forest, nourishment from the earth.
How about winter?
Only when you refuse to go out does winter exist.

In the sky above the lake, the star lights are twinkling.
Behold that tiny one.
Makes me recall the scene when kids came home,
How they helped remove weeds, talking and laughing along.
With warm yellow light, the star light is twinkling.

Behold the farther one.
As if big brother is talking to me,
My little sister, come to your big brother when you are in need.
With a touch of orange color, the star light is twinkling.

Behold the remote one.
As if seeing my big sister from afar,
Asking me not to gain weight each time we meet, yet keeps bringing food to me.
With a tender pink color, the star light is twinkling.

Behold that fading one.
Makes me recall the seniors of our clan,
Frequently fail to find red clothes, frequently fail to recall grandkids' names.
Yet keep on nagging, why not go to cook, for everyone to feel full.
With a misty gray concern, the star light is twinkling.

Behold the nearest one.
Makes me recall the poems I wrote for a loved one,
In songs I sing for him, words from the bottom of my heart.
Happiness of fresh red,
the star light is twinkling.

Yet, there're more.
Behold those remote distant ones.
As if seeing my father and mother up in the sky,
Watching their daughter to see, if she's done something good.
Accompanied by numerous golden constellations,
Along in the sky, twinkling and smiling, without a word.

In dark nights, the star lights are twinkling.
Shining reflections of various colors.
More sparkling than gold, the lake face.
Love from the bottom of my heart
Is like the mouth of the spring in the lake,
Gushing out
Into the gold of the autumn lake.

金色的寧靜

華語

我不知別人稱她什麼名
但　我一直將她稱為　寧靜湖
她溫柔恬靜
靜靜地陪在活水湖旁
不管別的地方是如何熱鬧做戲
她還是
安靜到連倒影裡的鳥聲
都聽得著
水面紋路輕輕地配合節奏
連微風都躡足走過

從旁邊的觀潮橋看過去
就是壯闊的太平洋
你會看到
黃昏時分　勇敢的人下海撒網打魚
你會看到
清晨時分　相愛的人牽手看日出

寧靜湖一年到頭　泉水湧出
看起來沒出口　又總是清澈如鏡
看起來無入口　又總是泉源不斷
雖然沒多大　但
花香不在多　湖靜何需大
這已經是我心中最美的湖了

湖水和星光
一起
走過春天、走過夏天
秋天呢？
秋天的蟬聲講著
和森林的緣分　和大地的生養
冬天呢？
冬天只會在你不想走出來時才有

湖面上空　星光閃啊閃
你看那粒細細的
讓我想起小孩回到家
會幫忙拔草　會一起有說有笑
星光將鵝黃色的溫暖　閃啊閃

你看那粒較遠的
像聽到兄長和我說
老妹，若有事要記得回來找阿哥喔
星光將橘子色的感動　閃啊閃

你看那粒有一點遠的
像看到遠方的阿姊
每次見面叫我不要再胖囉　還一直夾菜給我
星光將粉色的關心　閃啊閃

再看那粒微弱暗光的
讓我想起家族的老人家
時常找不到大紅色的衣服　時常叫不出子孫的名
還是叨唸~怎麼還不快去煮飯給大家吃飽來呢？
星光將灰濛灰濛淡黃色的不捨　閃啊閃

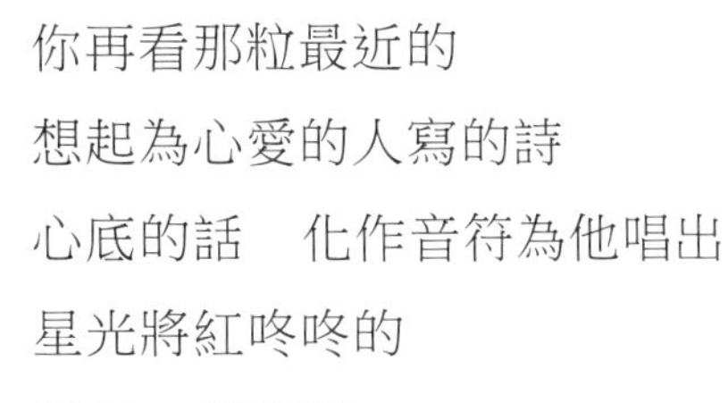

你再看那粒最近的
想起為心愛的人寫的詩
心底的話　化作音符為他唱出
星光將紅咚咚的
幸福　閃啊閃

還有還有
你再看那很遠很遠的
像看到阿爸阿姆在遠遠天上
總是看著女兒有什麼受讚許的事
旁邊很多很多的金色星群
全沒講話　陪在天邊笑咪咪　閃啊閃

暗夜星光一直閃
各種色一起映照下來
湖面比黃金還閃亮
心底的愛
就像湖裡的泉眼
湧出
秋湖在金色中

花色个大手帕巾仔

客語

一條花色个大手帕巾仔
包等飯篼仔
背在身項
陪𠊎去學校讀書
係一種
愛心

一條花色个大手帕巾仔
包等牲儀
擐在手項
陪㑇俚去伯公廟拜喏
係一種
保祐

一條花色个大手帕巾仔
包等笠嫲
戴在頭那頂
陪婦人家落田做事
係一種
煞猛

花色个大手帕巾仔
包等
美麗

水彩
39.5x27.2cm

~ Big Colorful Handkerchief ~

A big colorful handkerchief,
Wrapping a lunchbox,
Carried on my back,
Going with me to study at school.
That is
Love.

A big colorful handkerchief,
Wrapping the offerings,
Carried in my hands,
Going with me to worship at Pak Kung Temple.
That is
Blessing.

A big colorful handkerchief,
Wrapping a bamboo hat,
Worn on my head,
Going with me to work on the farm.
That is
Diligence.

The big colorful handkerchief
Is wrapping
Beauty.

花色的大手帕

華語

一條花色的大手帕
包著飯包
背在身上
陪我去學校讀書
是一種
愛心

一條花色的大手帕
包著牲禮
提在手上
陪我們去伯公廟拜拜
是一種
保祐

一條花色的大手帕
包著斗笠
戴在頭上
陪婦人家下田做事
是一種
勤勞

花色的大手帕
包著
美麗

月有情

客語

該日食小米酒
海風笑𠊎
係毋係想學李白酒後撈月
面紅濟炸个𠊎走去尋打魚郎
借網仔來撈酒醉个月光
手腳又趖人又戇戇
撈毋起一江明月
心肝肚又乜
撈起一簍公浪漫

同等金色羅帕个月光海
柔柔仔唱歌
享受平凡海浪正有个幸福
你逐日從太平洋跔起來
慢慢蹶上天頂
𠊎个思念
從海面上升

油畫
30F
91.0X72.5cm

月光在高高天頂眼看四方
夜色漸漸來到鹿鳴橋
月光就跈等偓行
陪偓轉夜
行過暗濛濛个綠色隧道
月光就從樹縫掖下
照光偓个路
夜幕奔下花東縱谷平原
月光就又跈等偓行
看等偓轉屋

有一種情
高掛天邊恬恬仔陪伴
有一種惜
帶等毋使講出个祝福
有時偓擎頭望月
就算你無看著
也微笑
像單純个小米酒甜到心肝肚
乜像天頂甜甜个月光

~ The Affectionate Moon ~

I was drinking millet wine, the other day.
At me, the sea breeze laughed,
Perhaps Li Bo I wanted to imitate, fishing for the moon when he was drunk.
To the fishermen I ran, with red face.
A net I borrowed, for fishing the drunken moon.
Clumsy and stupid,
A lake of moon, I couldn't catch.
Yet at the bottom of my heart,
A basket of romance had been caught.

Covered with a golden veil, the sea of moonlight.
Singing softly,
Enjoying the happiness, owned only by ordinary waves.
Up you rise, from the Pacific, everyday.
To the sky, you slowly mount.
My lingering thoughts,
From sea horizon, ascend.

High in the sky gazes the moon upon the world.
Slowly comes the night to Luming Bridge.
With me the moon walks,
Escorting me home late at night.
Passing the hazy green tunnel,
The moonlight sprinkles through the leaves,
Lighting the way I go.
Night's screen has covered the East Rift Valley.
The moon is following me,
Watching me go home.

There's a kind of affection,
A sweet company high in the sky.
There's a kind of mercy,
A blessing with no words.
At times up I raise my head, looking at the moon.
Even though you see not,
Yet I smile.
Like the simple millet wine, sweet to the bottom of my heart.
Which is also, like the sweet moon in the sky.

月有情

華語

那日喝小米酒
海風笑我
是不是想學李白酒後撈月
滿臉通紅的我跑去找打魚郎
借網子來撈酒醉的月兒
手腳笨拙　人又憨
撈不起一江明月
心底卻也
撈起一竹簍浪漫

披著金色面紗的月光海
輕柔歌唱
享受平凡海浪才有的幸福
你每天從太平洋起來
慢慢爬上天
我的思念
從海平面上升

月兒在高高天上眼看四方
夜色漸漸來到鹿鳴橋
月兒就跟著我走
陪我夜歸
走過暗濛濛的綠色隧道
月光就從樹縫撒下
照亮我的路
夜幕蓋下花東縱谷平原
月兒就又跟著我走
看著我回家

有一種情
高掛天邊甜甜的陪伴
有一種疼惜
帶著不必講出的祝福
有時我抬頭望月
就算你沒看到
也微笑
像單純的小米酒甜到心底
也像天上甜甜的月兒

山海戀

客語

山
一直恬靜過日仔
海
不時遊野通四方

包容、溫柔、彎彎斡斡个山
闊野野、勇敢、跑馬作浪个海
手牽手散步，從日頭行到臨暗
相愛个話語，從日出講到月落
逐日！過逐日！
像隔世相戀
又像生生世世个情緣
潮汐係愛个漣漪
漲潮時節係仰般个激情感動
退潮時節係仰般个戀戀不捨
傳唱愛情
畫出美麗个戀曲

Sui Ling
016.05

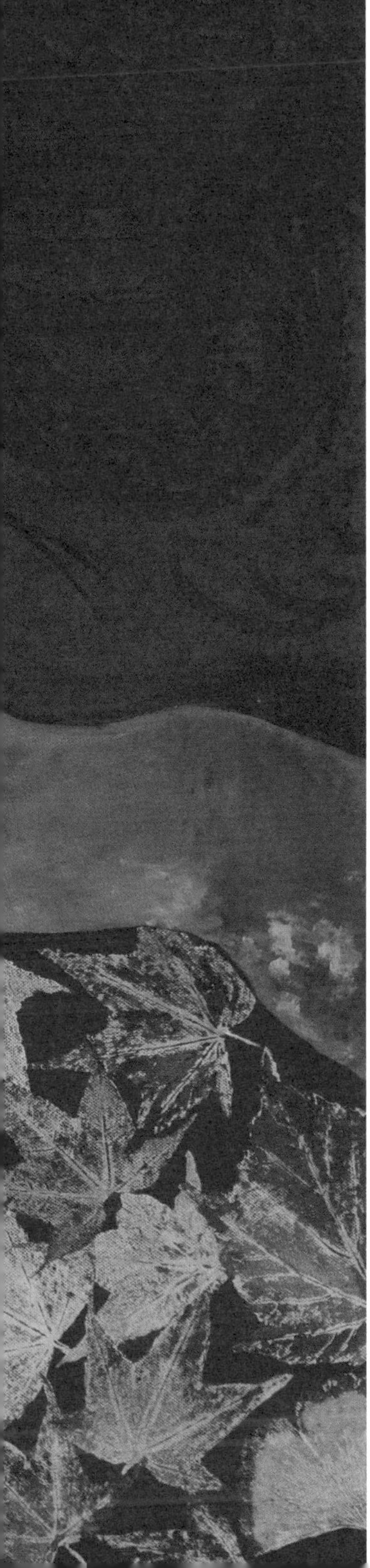

山海相戀
遠離世間脫離世俗
山，一日比一日，還較砸磳咧！
佢分人歡喜、分人偎凴！
海，一日比一日，還較靚咧！
佢餳人入心、餳人痛惜！

山摎海
就算濃情密意，想望相摘
毋過
山無可能分海包忒
海無可能摎山共樣恬靜
硬愛共樣
世界就毋會再過美麗

油畫
20F
72.5X60.5cm

愛人啊！愛人！
請分倨做自家
原來个倨，有不變个心
日頭、月光係證人
愛个美麗　　永久毋會消滅

山海相戀
毋單淨係一世情
係
千年萬年修鍊來个奇緣

~ Romance between the Mountain and the Sea ~

The mountain
Is always having his ordinary life.
The sea
Is often traveling around the world.

Tolerating and gentle, is the winding mountain.
Immense and brave, is the tumbling sea.
Taking a walk hand in hand, from bright sunlight to hazy dusk.
Speaking words of love, from sunrise to sunset.
Everyday! And everyday!
Like love between different lifetimes.
As if the endless love bonds, life after life.
Tides are the ripples of love.
How passionate and touching when tides rise.
How lingering and unwilling when tides fall.
Singing and passing of love songs,
Picturing beautiful songs of romance.

Romance between the mountain and the sea
Exists beyond the mundane world and secular vogue.
The mountain, stronger and stronger, day after day.
His grandeur, brings joys, brings trust!
The sea, more and more beautiful, day after day.
Her landscape, is appealing, is adorable!

The mountain and the sea,
With tender affection and sweet love, holding the same idea and hope,
Though,
The mountain could by no means be cocooned by the sea,
The sea could not possibly be peaceful as the mountain.
Insisting on one and the same,

The world shall be beautiful no more.
Oh, love! My love!
Allow me to be myself.
I, as I used to be, have a heart that never changes.
The sun and the moon are witnesses.
The beauty of love, forever lasts and fades not.

Romance between the mountain and the sea,
Not just love of a lifetime
But
A serendipity gained from cultivations of millennia.

山海戀

華語

山
一直寧靜過日仔
海
時常野遊通四方

包容、溫柔、蜿蜒的山
遼闊、勇敢、激盪的海
手牽手散步，從艷陽走到黃昏
相愛的話語，從日出講到月落
每日！又每日！
像隔世相戀
又像生生世世的情緣
潮汐是愛的漣漪
漲潮時是如何的激情感動
退潮時是如何的戀戀不捨
傳唱愛情
畫出美麗的戀曲

山海相戀
遺世絕俗
山，一日比一日，更壯碩了！
他的美，讓人歡喜、讓人仰仗！
海，一日比一日，更美了！
她的景，引人入勝、引人疼惜！

山與海
縱然濃情密意想望相同
不過
山不可能讓海包住
海不可能與山同樣寧靜
硬要一樣

世界就不再美麗
愛人啊！愛人！
請讓我做自己
原來的我，有不變的心
太陽、月兒是證人
愛的美麗　　永垂不朽

山海相戀
不只是一世情
是
千年萬年修鍊來的奇緣

一片真心／客語

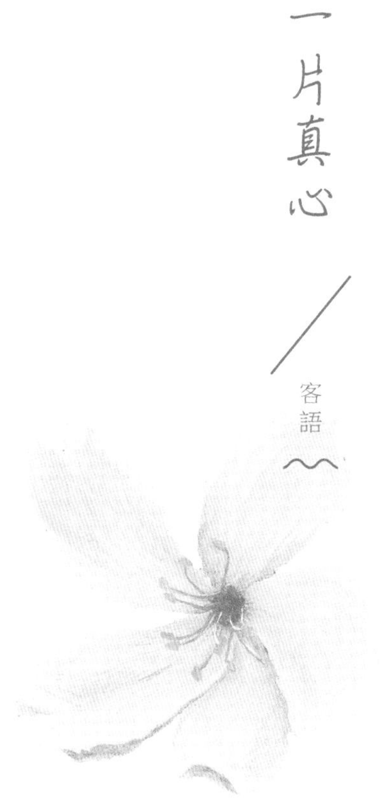

藍天毋會將好東西囥起來
佢分跈得著腳步个人看著
浸青个山林田園
有闊闊个心胸

土地毋會將好東西囥起來
佢分煞猛認分个耕種人看著
金色个飽滿禾串
有淰淰个豐收

桐花乜共樣
佢分有情有義个人看著
靚靚个花蕊
有一片真心

~ A True Heart ~

The blue sky would not hide any good things.
He allows them to be seen, by those who could catch up with him.
Fresh green forests and farms
Possess wide open minds.

The earth would not hide any good things.
He allows them to be seen, by cultivators who work hard and fulfill their duties.
Rich golden spikes of rice
Contain full harvests.

Likewise are tung blossoms.
Affectionate and faithful, they allow you to see,
The beautiful stamens
Containing a true heart inside.

油畫
6F
41.0X31.5cm

一片真心

華語

藍天不會將好東西藏起來
他讓跟得上腳步的人看到
青翠的山林田園
有開闊的心胸

土地不會將好東西藏起來
他讓勤勞認分的耕種人看到
金色的飽滿稻穗
有滿滿的豐收

桐花也一樣
他讓有情有義的人看到
美麗的花蕊
有一片真心

真花摎假花

客語

真真假假
共樣係靚靚个花
無麼个爭差
有一日
好心人講
屋下係放假花
感情會虛虛假假
正開始認真觀察

假花
做得放當久
放到毋記得去整理
無想到
身項个泥灰緊來緊賁
難怪心花毋會開

真花
做毋得放當久
知伊無幾日仔就會謝
特別會多看幾眼
逐日乜定著記得換水、整理
看伊緊開緊靚
心花就跈等開

真真假假
蹛塵摎習慣
盡像愛情

油畫
6P
41.0X27.0cm

~ True Flowers and Fake Flowers ~

True or fake,
Beautiful flowers as they are,
With no difference.
One day,
A good-hearted person said,
If fake flowers are set at home,
The feelings will become fake and false.
Since then did I start to carefully observe.

Fake flowers
Could be set for long,
To the extent that you forget to take care.
It turns out,
The dust piles thicker and thicker on them.
No wonder, the flowers of our hearts could blossom not.

True flowers
Could not be set for long.
Knowing they are going to fade, in a few days.
More looks at them we take, in a day.
So are clean water and arrangement offered, everyday.
The more beautiful they grow, as we see,
The flowers of our hearts start to blossom, along with them.

True and fake,
Dust or habit,
Exactly the same, as love.

真花與假花

華語

真真假假
同樣是美麗的花
沒什麼差別
有一天
好心人說
家裡若放假花
感情會虛虛假假
才開始認真觀察

假花
可以放很久
放到忘了去整理
沒想到
身上的泥灰越來越厚
難怪心花不會開

真花
無法放很久
知她沒幾日仔就會謝
特別會多看幾眼
每天也一定記得換水、整理
看她越開越美
心花就跟著綻放

真真假假
塵封與習慣
像極了愛情

你在該等麼个

客語

火車一枋一枋過
強強會拉走人个波螺皺風
乜一陣一陣過

月台項
清風輕輕吹起長纜纜个頭那毛
柔柔仔問
車仔過去咧喔
你在該等麼个

剪票口
細貓仔行兼頓恬个腳步
輕聲講
喵～
既經無人賣車單咧喔
你在該等麼个

水彩
39.5X27.2cm

係毋係
等想念个車枋
係毋係
等遠方个思念
一個無法交代个行程
就像車枋
無停

你看車頭脣
無意種下个台灣欒樹
將深秋个思念
紅到你心肝頭歸大遍

火車轟隆轟隆講
來去～　來去～
你還在該等麼个

~ For what Are You Waiting There? ~

Trains have passed, one by one.
Whirlwinds that almost blow people away
Have passed, one by one, too.

On the platform,
The breeze, touching the long hair gently,
Asks in a soft voice,
The train has passed.
For what are you waiting there?

At the boarding entrance,
A kitten, coming closer to the still standing feet,
Asks in a soft voice,
Meow~
No one is selling train tickets now,
For what are you waiting there?

Are you
Waiting for the train occupying your mind?
Are you
Waiting for someone you miss from far away?
An itinerary which could not be well explained,
Is like a train
That did not stop.

Behold what is next to the train station.
An accidentally planted Taiwan golden rain tree.
Bringing the deep autumn feeling of missing someone,
Into the bottom of your heart, saturated in red color.

Rattling clattering, the train addresses,
Let's go~ Let's go~
For what are you waiting there?

你在那兒等什麼

華語

火車一班一班過
幾乎會拉走人的旋風
也一陣一陣過

月台上
清風輕輕吹起長髮
柔柔的問
車子過去了喔
你在那兒等什麼

剪票口
小貓靠近駐足的腳步
輕聲說
喵～
已經沒人賣車票了喔
你在那兒等什麼

是不是
等想念的車班
是不是
等遠方的思念
一個無法交代的行程
就像車班
沒停

你看車站旁
無意種下的台灣欒樹
將深秋的思念
紅到你心底一整片

火車轟隆轟隆講
來去～　來去～
你還在那兒等什麼

做種个花

客語

紅色个蓮蕉花
跈新娘行嫁[1]
熟水个花枝層層包等畏羞
心中綻放紅色花蕊
在生命轉彎个旮旯角
用身項个流線
仰望天晴

毋管天寒風冷
寒天共樣有福蔭
毋管地旱日曬
行到哪位生到哪位

1 行嫁：出嫁。傳統結婚禮俗新娘準備嫁妝時必備蓮蕉花，繁殖力極強的植物，意指結婚後能多子多孫，客家老一輩俗稱「做種」。

佢　毋使掌聲 自家綻到半天高
向天開出啾紅

蓮蕉花問自家
麼个安到傳統？
蓮蕉花問自家
煞猛綻筍為了麼个？

佢摎自家講
能生存下去正做得成為傳統
佢摎自家講
愛煞猛綻出生命个靚　展現生命个流線
正係一場永恆个生命延續

油畫
6F
41.0X31.5cm

~ Flower of Fertility ~

Red canna lily,
Along with the bride, is married off.
Covered in layers, the mature twig flower.
Blossoming in the heart, the red stamens.
At the remote corner where life takes a turn,
By the streamline of the body,
Up she looks at the blue sky.

With cold air and chilly wind,
There is blessing of shade in winter days.
In the subathed dry land,
She grows wherever she lands.
Without applause, grows she to the midair.
Deep red she blossoms, to the sky.

To herself, the canna lily asks,
What is tradition called?
To herself, the canna lily asks,
What for to strive to sprout and spread?

To herself she replies,
Only when you survive could the tradition be complete.
To herself she replies,
Only when you strive to blossom the beauty of life, display the streamline of life,
Could an eternal life keep going on.

做種的花

華語

紅色的蓮蕉花
跟著新娘出嫁
成熟的花枝層層含蓄
心中綻放紅色花蕊
在生命轉彎的偏僻角落
用身上的流線
仰望晴天

不管天寒風冷
冬天一樣有福蔭
不管地旱日曬
走到哪裡長到哪裡
她　不必掌聲　自己長成半天高
向天開出深紅

蓮蕉花問自己
什麼叫做傳統？
蓮蕉花問自己
努力延展冒芽為了什麼？

她跟自己講
能生存下去才得以成為傳統
她跟自己講
要努力綻放生命的美　展現生命的流線
才是一場永恆的生命延續

禾桿人个心聲

客語

倨有腳　腳無法度停動
倨有嘴　嘴無法度講話
毋過　倨有目珠　看得到倨个世界
倨無別項才調
淨會看顧田園

美麗田園倨个家
煙囪下　醃缸　毛籣　磨石
磨出代代相傳　實在又鍚人个點心
腳底下　蜗仔　赤牛　田水
映出樣樣自然　煞猛又定貼个人生
日頭　月光　日到夜輪流守護
滿坪禾串係最靚个想望

水彩
39.5X27.2cm

毋知哪央時　人心起了一種魔幻
屋肚做得曬出人工日頭味
毋使畜豬就有豬油噴噴香
任在金錢魔力撮把戲

毋知哪央時　無定著有一種可能
禾該黃 水正落
飯該熟 火正著
等到靚靚家園變樣了
再多金錢再大魔力
乜買毋轉一坵一坵美麗田園偓个家

現下
長長个田園大道
企一頭大樹
樹影下茶壺仔
成了攝影機个主角
耕種人　成了鎂光燈个最愛
孩點心行田脣　成了壁頂相片肚个回憶

偓毋曾妄想
田園肚美麗公僕个稱說
淨想
毋管仰般變
禾浪翻飛永久係偓最靚个陪伴

~ Scarecrow's Words ~

I have feet, which could not move.
I have a mouth, which could not talk.
Yet, I have eyes, which could see the world of mine.
I have no other talents,
But watching the fields.

The beautiful farms, the home of mine.
Under the chimney are tanks of pickles, round bamboo baskets, and a millstone,
Making authentic and luring desserts, passed down generation by generation.
Underfoot are frogs, yellow cattle, and paddy fields,
Reflecting the diligent and stable life, natural in all aspects.
Guarded by the sun and the moon, in turns, from day to night,
Spikes of rice filling all the fields, is the best prospect.

Since when, no one knows. In human hearts, a magic grows.
Artificial smell of sun could be created, inside the house.
Aromatic lard for cooking could be made, without raising pigs.
By the power of money, tricks are played, as they like.

Since when, no one knows, might there come a kind of possibility.
The rain shall not fall until the harvest time of rice.
The fire shall not be lit until the rice is ready to be served.
Once the pretty homestead has lost its shape,
No matter how much money and how powerful the magic you call,
Blocks and blocks of gorgeous farms, my homeland, could not be regained.

Nowadays,
On the long field avenue,
Stands a big tree.
The tea pot under the shade,
Has become the star in front of cameras.
Farmers are adored by spotlights.
Carrying desserts by shoulder pole and walking on farm ridges,
has become a photo memory,
on the wall.

I dare not have any illusions
Of being praised by gorgeous civil servants in the fields.
Only a wish-
No matter what changes come this way,
The tumbling flying waves of paddy fields shall forever remain my best company.

稻草人的心聲

華語

我有腳　腳無法行動
我有嘴　嘴無法講話
但　我有眼睛　看得到我的世界
我沒其他才能
只會看顧田園

美麗田園我的家
煙囪下　醃菜缸　圓竹籃　石磨
磨出代代相傳　實實在在　又吸引人的點心
腳底下　青蛙　黃牛　水田
映出樣樣自然　勤勞又穩當的人生
太陽　月兒　白日到黑夜輪流守護
滿地稻穗是最美的想望

不知何時　人心起了一種魔幻
屋子裡可以曬出人工太陽味
不用養豬就有豬油香噴噴
任由金錢魔力變把戲

不知何時　或許有一種可能
稻子都到該收成時 才下雨
飯都到該煮熟了 火才點著
等到漂亮家園變樣了
再多金錢再大魔力
也買不回一方一方美麗田園我的家

如今
長長的田園大道
站一棵大樹
樹蔭下茶壺
成了攝影機的主角
耕種人　成了鎂光燈的愛慕
挑點心走田埂　成了牆上相片裡的回憶

我不曾妄想
田園裡美麗公僕的稱說
只想
不管如何變
稻浪翻飛永遠是我最美的陪伴

斷橋鄉魂

客語

共樣个日頭，無共樣个你
曾經係著等一領人人阿諛个藝術 品[1]
今這下身項嗄披等一領褪色个光陰衫
記錄等一擺過一擺天搖地動 山崩地裂
崩落个橋墩記憶等破碎个傷痛
古董个紅磚發出一息息強強敨毋轉氣个聲
風中像還略略仔聽著火車聲轟隆轟隆駛過來
像還聽到祖先个語言
向天請問 過往車枋 [2] 敢有帶走過往个痛腸

油畫
30F
91.0X72.5cm

1. 龍騰斷橋建於 1905 年，當時被稱為「台灣鐵路藝術極品」。
2. 在山線雙軌鐵路通車後，沿線舊有的鐵路及隧道也隨之走入歷史。

無共樣个容顏，無共樣个敨氣
無了軌道个殘缺靈魂在雲霧中跈等龍騰空遊野
遠眺 高擎擎又沈寂个無言
疑狐 綻到半天高个魚藤敢還係傳說中个魚藤[3]？
絡食个苦難 動搖了祖先个土地
失忒靈魂个客家人，敢還係客家人
行兼來 唚橋腳个必壢
撫慰遊子心頭个傷痕

3. 龍騰舊名魚藤坪，有「關刀斬魚藤，魚藤毒鯉魚」的傳說故事。

殘缺个靚留隻永久个窗口 看過去
有佢日夜思念个故鄉
埋在地泥肚个肚臍絆化做春泥
田園景色一幅過一幅還較靚　還較鬧
河壩水帶等野薑花香味　川流不息
滿係油桐子个地泥提醒佢
一粒有魂个種 會有淰淰个花開

佢恅著佢偷偷帶走佢个尊嚴　佢做佢
趕坐人生車枋走遠遠
毋過，無論走幾遠 飛幾高
暗夜發夢个場景還係該隻窗口肚看過去
个禾埕、山林、田坵、身影...
原來帶毋走个係　生根个鄉魂

~ Nostalgic Soul of the Broken Bridge ~

The sun, still the same. Different are you.
Dressed in an artwork praised by everyone, once upon a time.
Covered in a faded shirt of time, nowadays.
Recorded are earthquakes and landslides, time and again.
Torments of devastations are recorded in the broken bridge piers.
Faint panting breaths are gasped by the ancient red bricks.
Vague rumbling in the wind, sounds as if a train is coming in.
Lingering are words of ancestors,
Asking Heaven, whether the passing train has taken the sorrows of the past.

Different is the look, so is the breathing.
This soul is incomplete without a rail, wandering in the fog and cloud, chasing a dragon.
From afar I gaze upon the towering and solitary silence,
Wondering, whether the derris growing to midair is still that legendary derris.
The sufferings of making a living have shaken the ancestral lands.
Without soul, are Hakka people still Hakka?
Closer I walk, kissing the cracks of bridge piers,
Which soothed the scarred hearts of travelers.

The incomplete beauty has left an enduring window, through which I gaze upon the hometown I miss, day and night.
The umbilical cord buried deep down has transformed into spring soil.
The landscapes of farms are more beautiful and more splendid, one after another.
The river water carries the aroma of ginger lilies, flowing endlessly.
The soil full of tung tree seeds is reminding me,
A seed with soul shall be promised with flourishing blossoms.

Stealthily taking my dignity away, I thought. Rushing for the train of my life, to run far and away, as I like.
Yet, no matter how far and how high I have run,
The scenes of late night dreams, through that window, are still the rice grounds, the forests, the farms, the silhouettes...
So do I know, what could not be taken away is the rooted nostalgic soul.

斷橋鄉魂

華語

一樣的日頭，不一樣的你
曾經是穿著一件人人誇獎的藝術品
如今身上卻披著一件褪色的光陰衫
記錄著一次又一次天搖地動 山崩地裂
崩落的橋墩記憶著破碎的傷痛
古董的紅磚發出些微快要喘不過氣的聲音
風中好像還約略聽到火車聲轟隆轟隆駛過來
好像還聽到祖先的語言
向天請問過往車班是否已帶走過往的傷心

不一樣的容顏，不一樣的喘氣
沒了軌道的殘缺靈魂在雲霧中跟著龍騰空遊走
遠眺 高聳又沈寂的無言
心疑 長到半天高的魚藤是否還是傳說中的魚藤？
謀生的苦難 動搖了祖先的土地
失去靈魂的客家人，是否還是客家人呢？
走靠近 親吻橋墩的裂縫
撫慰遊子心頭的傷痕

殘缺的美留個永久的窗口
看過去 有我日夜思念的故鄉
埋在地底的臍帶頭化做春泥
田園景色一幅又一幅更美　更繁華
河水帶著野薑花香味　川流不息
滿是油桐子的地泥提醒我
一粒有魂的種 會有滿滿的花開

我以為我偷偷帶走我的尊嚴
任性的趕坐人生車班逃遠遠
但，無論逃多遠　飛多高
深夜做夢的場景還是那個窗口裡看過去的稻埕、山林、田園、身影...
原來帶不走的是　生根的鄉魂

返生个擔竿

客語

橫忒个老豬欄孤栖孤栖
唇口一堆泥糞
一陣大雨落過
顯出埋在地泥下个一枝擔竿

挖起沉睡个擔竿
仰般行過个時間挖再深
都挖毋轉
同屋下人共下汗流脈絡个回憶
合等目汁
流轉

水彩
39.5X27.2cm

本本硬程个圓身
左片个翿
紀錄等
�過一擔擔蕃薯摎豬菜
右片个翿
紀錄等
�過一缸缸大醃缸个水
扳頭摘頸个肩頭
為著生活打拚
為愛惜行過有情路
擔竿盡知

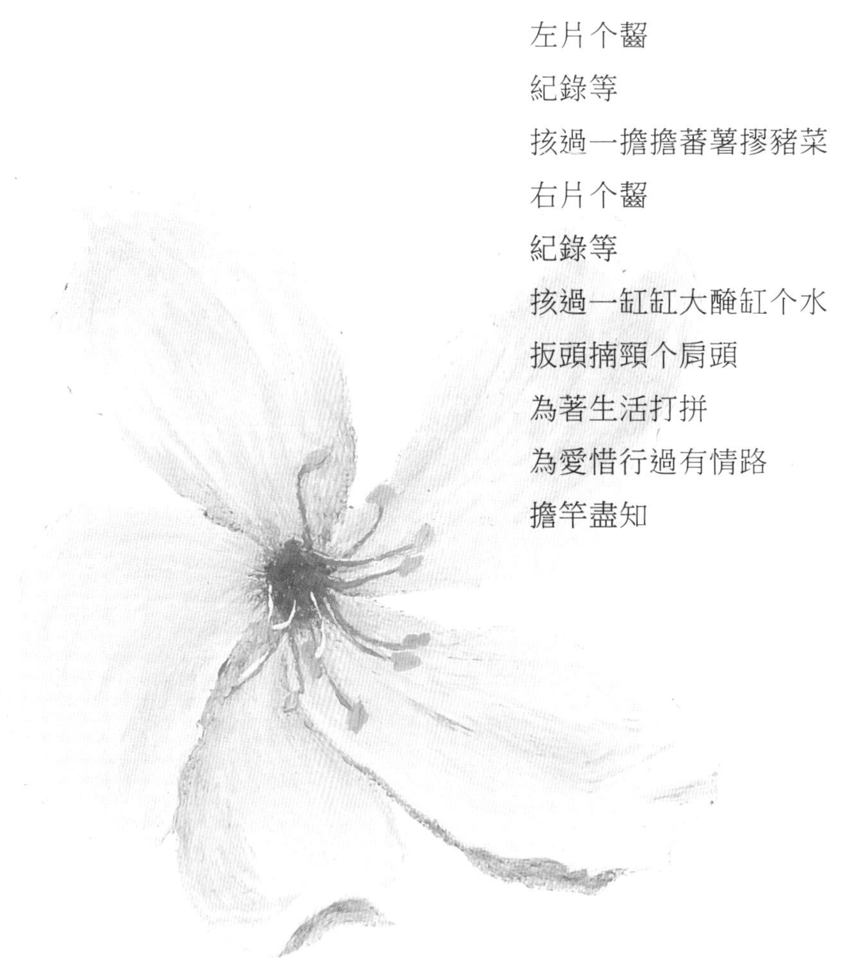

烏暗搕毋忒志氣
無擔好孩个擔竿
埋在地泥下　毋肯歿忒
煞猛打拚个硬頸
本本硬過擔竿

擔竿跖起來咧
跈等祖先个腳印
同放在雲頂高个科技
共下
做膽行人現代

~ Resurrection of the Shoulder Pole ~

Silent is the collapsed pig stall,
With a pile of mud next to it.
After a heavy rain,
Appears a buried shoulder pole under the ground.

Digging up the shoulder pole from his sleep,
Digging still deeper, why couldn't times past
be dug back?
The memory with my family, together soaked in sweat,
Mixed with tears
Is running.

Hard and strong, as it used to be.
Dent on the left end
marks
the baskets of sweet potatoes and pig feed.
Dent on the right end

marks

the tanks and tanks of water.

The shoulders of deep affections,

Striving to make a living,

Going through the way of love, for mercy and care.

The shoulder pole knows the best.

Darkness buries not dignity.

The shoulder pole with no baskets to carry,

Down under the ground, refuses to decay.

The hard neck of toil

Remains harder than the shoulder pole.

Up comes the shoulder pole.

Ancestors' footsteps does he follow,

Placed within the technology of cloud,

Altogether,

Bravely entering the modern world.

復活的扁擔

華語

倒下的豬舍孤單沉寂
旁邊一堆泥漿
一陣大雨下過
露出埋在地底下的一枝扁擔

挖起沉睡的扁擔
為何走過的時間挖再深
都挖不回
和家人一起汗流浹背的回憶
和著淚水
流轉

依舊硬朗的身軀
左邊的凹痕
紀錄著
挑過一擔擔蕃薯和豬菜
右邊的凹痕
紀錄著

挑過一缸缸大水缸的水
情感深厚的肩膀
為著生活打拼
為疼惜走過有情路
扁擔最知曉

黑暗掩埋不了志氣
沒擔可挑的扁擔
埋在地底下　不肯腐爛
勤勞打拼的硬頸
依舊硬過扁擔

扁擔爬起來了
跟著祖先的腳印
與放在雲端的科技
一起
做膽走入現代

燒暖个光

客語

赤腳嬤踏行在海灘
浪花冲走腳底个沙
一寸一寸摟空
無論在哪位
山林肚，抑係都市叢林
清心抑係茫心
矚目乜看得著一大遍闊野野个大海
潮起潮退　洋洋洋洋

手牽手
行過一波一波个浪潮
船來！船往！
毋管別人仰般看法，仰般多話
不變个心在海港等你

水彩
39.5X27.2cm

天邊海角　渺渺茫茫
天昏地暗　暗摸胥疏
係毋係　尋得著航向呢？
浩洪斗雨个時節　　看著分海風掀起个大海
百花盛開个時節　　眼前係一遍相思海
風吹日炙个人生
總有悲歡離合

燈塔企在人生个海港
佢有史詩个氣質，交響樂个撼動
有人生脈動个紀錄
有心靈个寫照
豐富个人生故事　餳旅客來到這位
有看著亮光个人就知
佢麼个都無，淨有一粒心
一粒有情有義个心

一條退休个船仔，一息都停動不得个船仔
停在無人个沙灘，無人過問
任憑海浪無情拍打，海風無情唛喊
行過个腳跡乜既經化為美麗波紋
成就大自然个靚

佢在遠方眺望
萬望創作共樣个歌、永恆个情
佢摎大海有隻約定
相約走尋共樣个歌、相知个心
堆疊 眼前个遼闊
撿拏人生
風光

月光下寫字
記憶个風化做
燈塔頂
一矖一矖燒暖个光

The Warm Light

Walking barefoot on the beach,
The waves are stealing the sand under my feet.
Inch by inch, empty.
No matter where I am,
In the forest, or inside the urban jungle,
Relaxed or disturbed,
An open sea I shall behold, once my eyes are closed.
Tides rise, tides fall, magnificent and immense.

Hand in hand,
Walking through waves and tides, one after another.
A boat comes! A boat goes!
No matter how others think and talk,
The unchanged heart is waiting, for you at the harbor.

The end of the sky and the edge of the sea, hazy and vague.
Dusky sky and gloomy earth, nothing but pitch-black.
Whether, the direction could be found?
In heavy rain, I behold the sea blown up by the winds.
In blooming seasons of flowers, I behold the sea of missing you.
The life blown by the wind and exposed to the sun
Contains sorrows and joys, farewells and reunions.

At the harbor of life stands the lighthouse.
He has the dispositions of an epic, the moving powers of a symphony.
He records the motions of life,
Reflects the images of heart.
By numerous stories of life, he attracts tourists to come here.
Those who see the light shall know,
He has nothing, but a heart,
An affectionate and faithful heart.

A retired boat, a boat incapable of moving,
Resting on the empty sand, nobody cares.
Though slapped by the relentless waves, shouted by the fierce winds,
His footsteps have transformed into beautiful water patterns,
Making the beauty of nature complete.

I gaze from afar,
Looking forward to creating songs of the same kind, feelings of eternity.
An agreement I have with the sea
Is looking for songs of the same kind, hearts of mutual understanding.
Building up, the immensity in front.
Collecting sceneries of
Life.

Writing under the moonlight,
The wind of memory has transformed
On the lighthouse
Into the sparkling warm lights.

溫暖的光

華語

打赤腳走在海灘
浪花冲走腳底的沙
一寸一寸淘空
無論在哪兒
山林裡，抑或都市叢林
清心還是慌亂
閉眼也看得著一大片遼闊的大海
潮起潮退　盛大寬廣

手牽手
走過一波一波的浪潮
船來！船往！
不管別人如何看法，如何多話
不變的心在海港等你

天涯海角　渺渺茫茫
天昏地暗　滿是漆黑
是否　找得到航向呢？
傾盆大雨時　看到被海風掀起的大海
百花盛開時　眼前是一片相思海
風吹日曬的人生
總有悲歡離合

燈塔站在人生的海港
他有史詩的氣質，交響樂的撼動
有人生脈動的紀錄
有心靈的寫照
豐富的人生故事　吸引旅客來到這裡
有看到亮光的人就知道
他什麼都沒有，只有一顆心
一顆有情有義的心

一艘退休的船，一點都動彈不得的船
停在無人的沙灘，無人過問
任憑海浪無情拍打，海風無情吶喊
走過的腳跡也已經化為美麗波紋
成就大自然的美

我在遠方眺望
殷切盼望創作同樣的歌、永恆的情
我與大海有個約定
相約找尋同樣的歌、相知的心
堆疊 眼前的遼闊
撿拾人生
風光

月光下寫字
記憶的風化做
燈塔上
一閃一閃溫暖的光

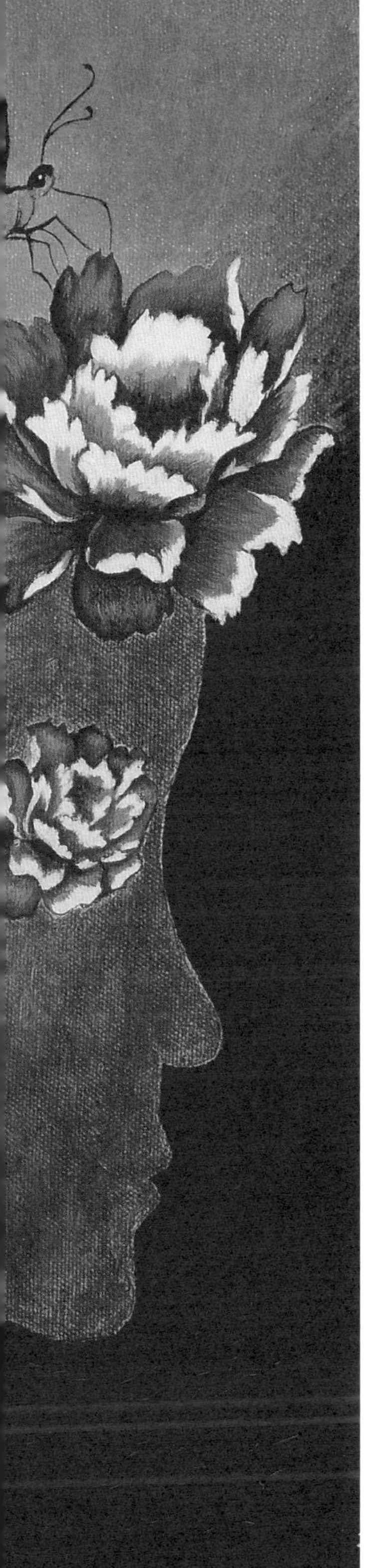

盛開个花

客語

四海為客个人
同天空 同河水 蒐集來个樸實
安然自在
印記在生命个長河

花仔一蕊一蕊
企好自家位所　展現自家个特色
每一個都各自堅強
每一儕都開到靚靚鬧鬧

揚蝶仔來了　揚蝶仔來了
看啊　滿園花開
揚蝶仔都飛等來了
無論在哪位
做一蕊煞猛盛開个花就著了

油畫
10F
53.0X41.0cm

~ Flowers in Full Blossom ~

World travelers,
Collect down-to-earth sincerity, from the sky, from the river.
At ease, satisfied and,
Imprinted in the long river of life.

One by one the flowers,
Well-poised in place, show individual characters.
Stern and strong, every one of them.
Thriving and gorgeous, every one of them.

Here come the butterflies! Here come the butterflies!
Behold the garden full of blooming flowers!
Flying butterflies, all arrive.
Wherever you are,
Just be a flower, always striving to blossom full.

盛開的花

華語

四海為客的人
向天空　向河水　蒐集來的樸實
安然自在
印記在生命的長河

花兒一朵一朵
站好自己崗位　展現自己的特色
每一個都各自堅強
每一位都開得美麗繁華

蝴蝶來了　蝴蝶來了
看啊　滿園花開
蝴蝶都飛著來了
無論在哪裡
做一朵努力盛開的花就對了

窩湖肚个秋

客語

四圍都係層層山崀
恬靜个細所在企在山腳下
秋風摎青山染色
黃、紅、柑……各種色
帶等各種心情

大樹下落葉無聲
心肝頭像跌忒當多講毋出个心事
一群細鳥仔從面前飛過
像飛起个落葉
閼開翼胛
撿起失落个心

水彩
54.5X39.5cm

毋驚
你看窩湖還裝等滿山滿谷个色目
田園肚个金黃色禾串
越來越飽滿
越來越罄頭
一坵一坵个菊花開容笑面
今年還係秋收浛浛

雖居山間
暗夜共樣有明月來照亮
朝晨共樣有日頭來喊醒
像花恁靚个揚蝶仔飛上飛下
河溪水為野薑花唱歌
在山肚唱出个真情
有山神加持
在山肚煞猛打拼个人
有天公爺痛惜

趕在天孿矄時節行出外背
想問麼儕較知秋滋味
鋒白个娘婆搖啊搖
請秋風代回答
秋係做得盡命牯開花个季節啊
打當結个文旦罄頭微笑
門口桂花無講話
回
一陣花香

~ Autumn in the Valley Plain ~

Surrounded by mountain ranges,
A small peaceful place stands at the foot of the mountain.
The autumn wind has dyed the mountain green
Into yellow, red, orange…… and other colors,
With moods of various kinds.

Leaves of big trees fall with no sound.
My heart feels profuse losses too great to tell
A flock of birds flies by,
Like the dancing fallen leaves,
Spreading their wings,
Lifting the fallen lost heart.

Fear not,

Behold the colors of the valley plain, filling all the mountains and valley.

The golden spikes of rice in the fields,

More and more stuffed have they become,

Lower and lower their heads hang down.

Blocks and blocks of Chrysanthemums smile ceaselessly.

A full autumn harvest, this year, is expected again.

Residing between mountains,

The bright moon comes to shine, the same in the night.

The sun comes to wake us up, the same in the morning.

Up and down fly the butterflies, beautiful as flowers.

The streams sing for ginger lilies.

True affections they sing out, in the mountains.

With the support of the Mountain God,

Hard-working people in the mountains

Are cherished by Heaven.

Out they rush at dawn.
Who knows better the autumn smell?
The snow white silver grasses sway,
Asking autumn wind to answer.
Autumn could be a season with blooms of flowers.
The fruit-laden pomelos droop their heads smiling.
With no words, the osmanthus by the doorway
Answers
With a spell of floral scent.

山谷平原裡的秋

華語

四周都是層層山巒
寧靜的小地方站在山腳下
秋風把青山染色
黃、紅、橘……各種色
帶著各種心情

大樹下落葉無聲
心頭像丟失很多無法講出的東西
一群小鳥從前面飛過
像飛起的落葉
展翅
掀起失落的心

不用怕
你看山谷平原裡還裝著滿山滿谷的色彩
田園裡的金黃色稻穗
越來越飽滿
越來越垂下頭
一區一區的菊花笑意綿綿
今年還是滿滿秋收

雖居山間
夜晚一樣有明月來照亮
清晨一樣有太陽來喊醒
似花美麗的蝴蝶飛上飛下
溪水為野薑花唱歌
在山裡唱出的真情
有山神加持
在山裡努力打拼的人
有上天疼惜

趕在曙光乍現時走出戶外
想問有誰更知曉秋的滋味
雪白的芒草搖啊搖
請秋風代回答
秋是可以盡情開花的季節啊
果實累累的文旦垂頭微笑
門口桂花沒講話
回
一陣花香

想望

客語

戴在山肚
開山打林，翻山過嶺
從來就毋會唉唉嘖嘖
仰愛恁樣
在這位，毋去別位呢
係跈等祖先个腳步
係歸圓身本來就流等煞猛打拼毋驚吃苦个血脈

戴在海唇
駛船打撈，餐風食露
從來就毋會打卵退
仰愛恁樣
在這位，毋去別位呢
係跈等魚仔个路線
係歸圓身本來就流等冒險患難勇敢向前个血脈

Sui Ling
2016.05

戴在街市
衝上衝下，無閒直掣
從來就毋會放棄
仰愛恁樣
在這位，毋去別位呢
係跈等社會个變化
係歸圓身 本來就流等買賣算分毋驚蝕本个血脈

山 擎得起
海 跼毋核
街市 毋驚競爭
全都想望
尋一種生活个力量

壓克力
50.0X37.5cm

Yearnings

Living in the mountains,
Cultivating forests, over peaks and across hills.
Neither groan nor sigh has ever been heard.
Why
Here, not elsewhere?
It's the steps of ancestors do I follow.
It's the blood of perseverance and endeavor that flows in the whole body of mine.

Living by the sea,
Sailing and fishing, dining in the wind and drinking with the dew.
Neither cowardice nor fear has ever taken over.
Why
Here, not elsewhere?
It's the routes of fish do I follow.
It's the blood of adventure and bravery that flows in the whole body of mine.

Living in the city,

Rushing here and there, hectic and frenetic.

Never has the thought of giving up come to mind.

Why

Here, not elsewhere?

It's the changes of society do I follow.

It's the blood of trading and daring that flows in the whole body of mine.

Achievable, is the mountain.

Boundless, is the sea.

Competitive, is the city.

All are yearnings

For a power of living.

想望

住在山裡
開墾山林，翻山越嶺
從來就不會哀聲嘆氣
為什麼
在這裡，不去別處呢
是跟著祖先的腳步
是全身本來就流著努力打拼不怕吃苦的血脈

住在海邊
行船打撈，餐風食露
從來就不會退縮畏懼
為什麼
在這裡，不去別處呢
是跟著魚的路線
是全身本來就流著冒險患難勇敢向前的血脈

住在城市
衝來衝去，百般忙碌
從來就不會放棄
為什麼
在這裡，不去別處呢
是跟著社會的變化
是全身本來就流著買賣算分不怕蝕本的血脈

山　舉得起
海　侷限不住
城市　不怕競爭
全是想望
找尋一種生活的力量

文學奇緣个大戲

客語

時間做大導演
他用獨有个思想主導這場戲
選了大路關个場景
兩百零年前邀請了一群客家子民
來到這位　開山打林
來到這位　深耕綻筍

老屋跡捲手寫腳本
一磚一瓦寫等
疲爬極蹶建立家園个過程
在眠床下个大醃缸寫等
煞猛種菜　揤覆菜　滷鹹菜个生活
在大禾埕个凳頭項寫等
打嘴鼓打鬥敘个情景，讀書講古个身影

油畫
30F
91.0X72.5cm

在井水水面寫等
阿太个阿太...活水个源頭
在天邊个雲彩寫等
大家係
仰般个緣分

藍天白雲田坵山林係最湛个布幕
純樸係大襟衫項靚靚个共樣个色水
钁頭鍚來攝影機个大鏡
挖出一坵一坵个禾秧
擔竿鍚來攝影人个目珠
孩出一擔一擔个穀糧
花色大手帕巾仔擦等流水樣仔个汗臊
日頭下笠嫲花開等...笑容

荒田無人耕，耕了有人爭
無想到遠遠來了鴨嬷王
連累歸遍客家莊
家園強強會分人滅忒去
客家六堆大團結
鄉親圍起右堆庄
盡命牯保護家園

大導演講：
歷史大戲無恁該就煞棚
覆菜塞到罐仔肚毋會生菇
囥在眠床下个老菜脯
越久越有搭碓
目珠擘金敨大氣就會知
大導演最合意个
在這位
連愛情都演到恁有老味緒

1915 年
時間大導演
再安排一位主角在這位出世
比原鄉人還較原鄉人
佢用多情个心
多采个文筆記錄
傳奇

這下
時間大導演
又用佢特別个眼光
邀請偲俚來到大路關
原來
這位所毋單淨係欣賞客家文學个關口
乜係前往台灣文學个大路
文學奇緣
正愛開始

~ The Big Drama of Literary Serendipity ~

The big director is time,
Who directs this drama by his unique way of thinking.
Choosing Daluguan as the scene,
He invited a group of Hakka people, two hundred years ago,
To come here, to cultivate the wasteland.
To come here, to be deep-rooted and sprout.

The old house had lent a hand writing script.
With every brick and tile writing
The passing hardships and struggles which built the homestead.
Under the bed, big pickle tanks writing
The assiduous life of growing vegetables, drying vegetables, and making pickles.
On the grain-drying ground, the stools writing,
The scenes of gathering and chatting, the silhouettes of studying and story-telling.
The surface of the well water writing

The source of flowing water, from great-grandfather of great-grandfather.
The colorful cloud in the sky writing,
Everyone was connected
By what kind of fate and destiny.

The blue sky and white cloud, the field and forest, together made the best screen.
Frugality was the same bright color on Hakka shirts.
A hoe had attracted the big lens of the camera.
Dug out were seedlings, piece by piece.
A shoulder pole had caught the eyes of the photographer.
Carried out were baskets of grains, one by one.
Wiped off was the smell of trickling sweat, by a big colorful handkerchief.
Under the sun, the bamboo hat was blossomed with a smiling face.

Uncultivated, a wasteland. Cultivated, people fought to take.
Unexpectedly came the Duck King from afar,
Causing miseries to the Hakka village as a whole.
Nearly annihilated, the homeland.
United were the six forces of Hakka tribes.
Sieging Rhiudoi Village, the country folks,
Fought to protect their homeland until they died.

Said the big director,
The historical drama would not end that easily.
Dried vegetables would get no mold inside the bottles.
Old dried radish preserved under the bed
Would get tastier the longer it sits.
With open eyes and a deep breath, you would know
The favorite of the big director
Was over here.
Even love was performed, in such an old way.

In the year of 1915
Time, the big director,
Here arranged a protagonist to be born.
More native than My Native Land.
With an affectionate heart,
Excellent writing skills, recorded he,
Legends.

Nowadays
Time, the big director,
Is applying the unique insight of his.
By inviting us to Daluguan,
He lets us know.
This is not a gate for appreciating Hakka literature only,
But a broadway to Taiwan literature, too.
The literary serendipity
Is about to begin.

文學奇緣的大戲

華語

時間做大導演
他用獨到的思想主導這場戲
選了大路關[1]的場景
兩百多年前邀請了一群客家子民
來到這裡　開墾荒地
來到這裡　深耕發芽

老屋幫忙寫腳本
一磚一瓦寫著
艱辛奮鬥建立家園的過程
在床鋪下的大醃缸寫著
勤勞種菜　做福菜　醃製鹹菜的生活
在曬穀場的板凳上寫著
聊天聚敍的情景，讀書講故事的身影
在井水水面寫著
曾祖父的曾祖父...活水的源頭
在天邊的雲彩寫著

1 大路關：屏東的一處古地名，鍾理和文學家的老家位於此。

大家是
怎樣的緣份

藍天白雲田園山林是最好的布幕
純樸是大襟衫上亮麗的同樣的色彩
鋤頭吸引攝影機的大鏡
挖出一片一片的秧苗
扁擔吸引攝影人的眼睛
挑出一擔一擔的穀糧
花色大手帕擦著流水般的汗臭
日頭下斗笠花開著…笑容

荒田無人耕，耕了有人爭
沒想到遠遠來了鴨母王
連累整個客家莊
家園幾乎快被人消滅
客家六堆大團結
鄉親圍起右堆庄
盡全力抵死保護家園

大導演說：

歷史大戲沒這麼簡單就演完

福菜塞到罐仔裡不會發霉

藏在床舖下的老菜脯

越久越有意思

眼睛睜大深呼吸就會知

大導演最喜愛的

在這裡

連愛情都演得這麼有老味道

1915 年

時間大導演

再安排一位主角在這裡誕出

比原鄉人[2]還原鄉人

佢用多情的心

多采的文筆記錄

傳奇

---

2 這裡指的是文學家鍾理和，以前有一部電影~原鄉人，就是他的故事。

現在
時間大導演
又用他特別的眼光
邀請我們來到大路關
原來
這地方不只是欣賞客家文學的關口
也是前往台灣文學的大路
文學奇緣
正要開始

海景隨想

客語

海石鞋

鞋 恬恬企在海脣

浪走遍天邊海角

從來都毋使愁 浪毋再來

這位係紅佳夢[1]之鄉

用等待个心情

享受

轉頭轉角堵著个甜蜜浪漫

用歲月个腳跡

記憶

割捨毋忒个愛戀

1 紅佳夢：台東富岡被稱為紅佳夢之鄉

2020.10

你知無？
石頭乜有感情
你聽著無？
偓个心來自太平洋

<u>海石胖凳</u>

胖凳恬恬坐在海唇
海風還係吹等

從來都毋使掛吊無人客
這位係巴沙哇力[2]

用你个細胞
摸
海个體溫

2 巴沙哇力：阿美族部落，字義為「向東方」

水彩
39.5X27.2cm

用你个胸膛

聽

風个心

你知無？

石頭乜有熱情

你聽著無？

偃个祝福來自太平洋

海舞

手髀擎高高，迎流瀉个月光

頭那臥高高，看緊矚个星光

柔情在身體流動

心肝肚激情飯滾浮鑊蓋

手
浪樣仔環車觔斗

胸
像海恁闊

心
多情深過海

手指頭
摎海對話

微笑
摎你共舞

~ Sea View Caprices ~

Sea Rock Shoe

The shoe stands silently by the sea.
The waves have traveled through the world.

It has never been worried, that the waves shall come no more.
For here is the home of Hongjiameng.

With the mood of waiting,
Enjoy
The sweet romance of meeting someone.

By the footprints of time,
Remember
The sentimental attachment that persists with no regret.

Do you know?
Rocks have feelings, too.
Could you hear?
From the Pacific Ocean does my heart come.

<u>Sea Rock Sofa</u>

Silently sits the sofa by the sea.
Waiting as the sea wind blows.

It has never been worried for lack of customers.
For Basawali is over here.

Use your cells
To touch
The temperature of the sea.

Use your chest
To listen
To the heart of the wind.

Do you know?
Rocks have passions, too.
Could you hear?
From the Pacific Ocean does my wish come.

Sea Dance

High raise the arms, welcoming the flowing moonlight.
High raises the head, looking at the shining stars.

Flow the tender feelings inside the body.

Tumble the passionate feelings on the bottom of the heart.

The hands
Are tumbling like the waves.

The chest,
Is expanding like the sea.

The heart,
Contains affections deeper than the sea.

The fingers,
Are talking to the sea.

Smiling
And dancing with you.

海景隨想

華語

海石鞋

鞋　靜靜地站在海邊
浪走遍天涯

從來都不必愁　浪不再來
這裡是紅佳夢之鄉

用等待的心情
享受
邂逅的甜蜜浪漫

用歲月的腳跡
記憶
纏綿不悔的眷戀

你知否？
石頭也有感情
你聽著否？
我的心來自太平洋

海石沙發

沙發靜靜地坐在海邊
海風還係吹等

從來都不必擔心沒客人
這裡是巴沙哇力

用你的細胞
摸
海的體溫

用你的胸膛
聽
風的心

你知否？
石頭也有熱情
你聽著否？
我的祝福來自太平洋

海舞

手臂舉高高，迎流瀉的月光
頭仰高高，看閃耀的星辰

柔情在身體流竄
激情在心底澎湃翻滾

手
浪樣般翻滾

胸
似海遼闊

心
多情深過海

手指頭
與海對話

微笑
與你共舞

作者介紹

彭歲玲

原籍苗栗三義，台東大學華語文學系台灣語文教育碩士，國小教職退休後，持續著力於客家文化及語言的傳承，現任客家委員會委員，客語薪傳師、講客廣播電臺主持人。

喜愛文學與繪畫，客語文學作品曾多次獲獎如：桐花文學獎、教育部閩客語文學獎、客家筆會創作獎、六堆大路關文學獎、苗栗文學集入選出版等。參與客家女聲女詩人團隊吟詩展演，喜歡創作及吟唱客語詩分享客語之美。

現居台東，專注創作，也帶領孩童創作詩畫及童話繪本。

一、個人繪本作品有：《雲火龍》、《阿三妹奉茶—添丁亭、膨風茶、礱糠析》、《沙鼻牯》。

二、師生合著作品有：《蟻公莫拉侄 - 客華雙語童詩童畫集》、細人仔狂想童話集系列《來尞喔》、《湛斗喔》、《當打眼》、《毋盼得》。

作者相關參考資訊請搜尋關鍵字「靚靚山海戀」，或掃描 QR Code。

《沙鼻牯》

這本故事繪本是澎澎老師和小兒子的親子創作合集，內含兩個小故事，《岐嶷个阿定牯》小故事中看見人與人之間的真情互動，《細黃狗》流浪狗的際遇牽動關懷社會的心。內文以客英華多語呈現，客英雙語的 QR Code 有聲書，苗栗縣政府 108 年出版。

《蟻公莫拉侄》客華雙語童詩童畫集

澎澎老師帶著一群小朋友寫自己的詩，畫自己的詩，本書集結了師生及 38 位大小作者的詩畫作品，極富天真童趣，本書錄製師生以客語朗讀自己詩作，以 QR Code 附錄於每篇詩文，增進語言風采及學習功效。

《阿三妹奉茶 - 添丁亭、膨風茶、礱糠析》

這三本系列套書是彭歲玲 (澎澎老師) 圖文創作的繪本客英雙語有聲書，以一個小女孩的日常生活為主軸，描述客家人的奉茶情景，呈現常民生活中體貼及充滿愛心的溫馨人情味，以傳承珍貴的客家文化及語言。

故事內文以客語，英文及華語呈現，每頁均有 QR Code 便於學習語音。

《雲火龍》

這本故事繪本是澎澎老師的文圖創作，雲火龍是客家莊的傳說故事，述說草龍身上插滿祈福香，在濛沙煙裡來回穿梭，在火焰中騰雲顯靈，為村民帶來好運。

故事內容是以客語及英文呈現的有聲書 (右翻學客語 , 左翻學英語)，附翻譯及客語拼音，並附錄 CD 以及 QRCODE 便於讀者學習，苗栗縣政府 106 年出版。

2017 年出版第一本
《來尞喔 !》

2018 年出版第二本
《湛斗喔 !》

2019 年出版第三本《當打眼》 2020 年出版第四本《毋盼得》

《細人仔狂想童話集》

這些系列作品是全國首創由孩童們分工合作構想故事、繪畫完成的客語故事繪本，是澎澎老師每年帶著一群來自不同學校的一群孩童一起創作的成果，濃濃客家味的繪本，來自於孩子們的想像世界，生動有趣，每頁均附 QR Code 便於語音學習，並附錄翻譯及客語拼音，內含三至四個有趣的故事，其中，《當打眼》《毋盼得》是客英有聲書，推廣雙語學習。

後 記

這輩子最勇敢的事，就是創作！

我在純樸的客家小山村長大，哥哥姊姊都比我大很多歲，同學鄰居也都住很遠，印象中小時候的自己話不多，國中時期更要走很遠的路才能坐到車去學校讀書，那時的我也很內向，讀師專時到了台南大都會，也是屬於較沒自信且不多言的人，一直到了當老師，不得不站在講台多講話，才將內向隱藏，慢慢從害羞到開朗。

走著走著，再回頭關注自己時，發現越是不講話，內心越是澎湃。中年之後突然覺得詩是很好的傾訴對象，尤其是以自己的母語來表達，用最親切的語言書寫自己的情感生命，感覺更可以載滿我的情懷，於是開始寫詩。詩的特色是省略很多描繪，留下的空白反而裝進許多想像，也重新彩色了我從小的內向，雖然我還很需要學習。

後來發現畫圖也是一種很美的表達，就嘗試開始繪畫創作，除了自已畫繪本，也帶領孩童們創作詩畫及繪本故事，邊創作邊累積感動，於是產出了這本詩畫選集。也因為受到華哥的影響及鼓舞，於是又異想天開，學著將創作的詩，唱成了歌。後來發現唱歌更有感覺，原來情緒可以更抒發，沒想到稚嫩的拙拙的唱法，竟然也做成 MV 可以分享。

這些表達方式對我來說，並不專業，可稱素人吧！全都因為喜歡就開始了，所以覺得自己真的很勇敢。

感謝生命中遇見的貴人，給予很大鼓勵，承蒙美惠老師一路以來的繪畫指導；音樂製作的威龍老師鼓勵我們，保留這種非專業的聲音最珍貴；金曲歌手思容幫忙作曲，也教我唱歌技巧；感謝同事欣怡犧牲連假幫我打樂譜，怡汝和 John-Michael 和曉婷在英文專業的協助，還有 Rita 和婉鈞的大力幫忙；感恩親愛的家人，還有好多朋友的支持鼓勵，很感恩生命中遇見你們！

此書收錄 24 首詩，是挑選這幾年來自己最有感動的作品，一字一句是對自己的誠實面對，詩寫心情，是情感的紀錄也是夢想的實現。其中有五首唱成歌，譜出樂譜，當中的三首由小兒欣展拍成了 MV。因為想保留珍貴的母語及提升母語的國際價值，因此，每篇都有附客語及英語的 QR Code 音檔，三首 MV 也同樣附上 QR Code，歡迎閱聽我雖不成熟卻是最勇敢、最真摯的表達。

詩歌畫選集的出版，純粹想分享，若聽到有人喜歡就覺得開心！鐵花村的音樂總監鄭捷任鼓勵大家創作時説過「好的曲子，自己會長腳。」所以我就充滿想像，真希望書裡的詩歌會生出很多很多腳，到處跑，倘若作品能帶給人一些些感動，此生足矣！

國家圖書館出版品預行編目 (CIP) 資料

記得你个好：詩畫選集(含樂譜/MV) = Your goodness is always on my mind / 彭歲玲著.
-- 初版. -- 臺東市：澎澎工作室, 2020.11
224 面；20x21 公分
ISBN 978-986-99814-0-8(精裝)

863.51　　　　109019155

指導贊助：文化部 MINISTRY OF CULTURE
圖文創作者：彭歲玲
英文翻譯：呂曉婷
英語錄音：John-Michael L.Nix
英文校稿：劉怡汝
客語錄音：彭歲玲
音樂作曲：羅思容、許良華
音樂製作：張威龍
影像製作：許欣展
樂譜製作：吳欣怡
繪畫指導：江美惠
油畫協力：Rita Su 蘇文惠
設計編輯：玢紛玩設計 - 廖婉鈞
QR 製作：陳玉萱
封面題字：陳一郎

出版：澎澎工作室
發行人：彭歲玲
地址：臺東市北平街 63 號
電話：089351046
電子信箱：ponling4840@gmail.com
初版：2020 年 11 月
定價：新臺幣 500 元